GETTING LUCKY

A STEAMY ST. PATRICK'S DAY NOVELLA

SARAH SPADE

A TRIP TO BOSTON

Maddie

"Ah, shit. I forgot all about it!"

My head's in the oven when Sheila's voice rings out in our brand new, state of the art, massive kitchen. She's not too far from me, working on some dough a couple of counters over, and I can hear the aggravation in her tone as she pounds the stainless steel countertop with her hands.

I finish tapping the tops of the muffins I'm checking—they don't spring back so I know they're not ready yet—and pull my head out of the oven in time to see Sheila scowling up at her boyfriend, Cole. He has his hands out apologetically, a real *don't shoot the messenger* gesture, and I figure that whatever Sheila forgot, Cole must have just reminded her about it.

I love Sheila dearly. She's my business partner, as well as one of my closest friends. And if she sprung anyone else on me as our third employee because she was sleeping with him, I'd throw them both out of my kitchen. Luckily for them, since they've become a serious item a couple of weeks ago, I've started to get used to Cole. He's good for her, keeping her frantic, whirlwind of a personality in check.

Besides, he's the one who technically owns our new kitchen. He's not my boss, because Sheila and I agreed years ago to be equal partners, but he holds the mortgage for this amazing new home for our catering business. For that alone, he gets a pass.

But he really is good for Sheila. She picks up the nearby rolling pin, smacking her dough in order to get out her frustrations, while Cole murmurs something softly under his breath to her. Her scowl seems to melt off of her pretty face. After tossing the rolling pin to the side, she shoves her flour-coated hands back in the dough, kneading it angrily. At least she isn't beating it up anymore.

I quirk my eyebrow over at her. "Everything okay, Sheila?"

"Yeah. Sorry, Maddie. I forgot about a supply pick-up, but it's okay. Cole's got an easy fix for me." Still working her dough, she uses her hip to bump into his. "Hey, babe. Since I'm tit's deep in sourdough, can you call him, make sure the order's ready? I put the number in your phone."

At Sheila's request, Cole pulls out his cell phone, frowning at it as he shifts it in his palm. "I don't know how you girls do it. I'll never get used to this shape."

I look over at his phone. It's an iPhone, one of the newer models, and while the screen is kind of big, it's the same shape as every other iPhone out there.

Sheila catches me looking at him curiously. With a shrug, she explains, "He used to have an Android."

My nose wrinkles. Oh. He's one of *those* people.

As Cole wanders off to have some privacy for his phone call, I turn back to see that, instead of kneading her dough, Sheila's still watching me. Only she's not smirking at the fact that I'm a diehard Apple fan or that I think Cole should've switched over long before now. No. It's... it's *that* look again.

I feel my back go up. "What?"

"Nothing, sweetie."

Nothing? Yeah, right. Sheila's been doing this for weeks. She keeps looking at me with this sad expression, like she's gotten bad news and doesn't know how to tell me. What makes it worse is that Sheila Walsh is one of the most honest, open people I know. Even when she went into that funk before Cole came back, I knew it had to do with a guy she was hung up on. I got to hear all about her impulsive road trip with a stranger and how she was convinced he was the real deal instead of—as she so charmingly put it—a "one and done".

She *never* holds anything back.

To see her wearing that look every time I turn around in the kitchen? It's beginning to spook me.

I'd rather ask her about this pick-up. "What's the call about? What did you forget?"

"What? Oh. Right. You know that catering gig we have next weekend?"

"Yeah. The McGuire's are hosting a retirement party at the VFW. I booked that gig."

"Right. And they requested Guinness bread and a beef stew. See where I'm going with this?"

I nod. Since it was my job to take inventory of all of our pantry staples when we first relocated to the new kitchen, I know exactly what Sheila is saying. Guinness bread is one of our local specialties and, for some reason, Sheila won't run down to the liquor store for a can. As stubborn as Sheila is, I've learned long ago when to pick my battles. If she says that she can only make a loaf with the brew from one particular Irish pub, fine.

Except we didn't have any of Finnegan's Guinness when I loaded the pantry.

"You were supposed to pick up some more alcohol from that pub you like?"

"Yup. I ordered four cases last week and Finn told

me to give him a couple of days to get the order together. I was supposed to go pick it up and I forgot. I don't know where my head's been at. I only just remembered Finn said he was leaving the country soon. He's going on vacation and he needed us to pick that beer up before he goes."

I don't even bother asking about using another type of beer. Sheila won't have it, and then I'll have to listen to her go on and on why that one particular pub's Guinness is the only Guinness she'll use.

Sheila picks up her dough, tosses it, then slams it back on the countertop. Flour explodes into the air, covering her apron and turning her caramel-colored skin a ghostly pale. She kneads it again with so much force, it's like she thinks the sourdough has something to do with why she forgot.

I leave her to it, returning to my oven to check on the muffins. They're done and, this time, I pull them out, put them on the cooling rack. I go over to my stand mixer to scoop out another batch just as Cole finishes his call.

"Okay, ladies. I have good news and bad news. Good news is I talked to one of the guys who works at Finnegan's and he says that the order is there. The bad news is that, as busy as it's been there lately, he's not so sure how much longer they can hold onto it. They're running low, too."

"So we have to get it now."

Cole nods.

"Let me finish up with this," Sheila says, slapping her dough a few more times for good measure, "then I guess we can take the ride into Boston together."

I don't see why the two of them need to go. I mean, I understand *why* they would. Of course, Sheila wouldn't send Cole into Boston by himself, and their relationship is too new for her to feel comfortable leaving him behind. I get it. It might have been, well, years since I've had a serious relationship like theirs, but I get it. They're still in the honeymoon stage. Of course, they'd go together.

But that's wasteful. And kind of ridiculous. My muffins I'm working on are basically done and I can leave them for Cole to bake. Sheila's just getting started on her sourdough, and that's not counting the prep she wanted to start for some of the short orders we have this week.

"Don't be silly. I can go."

"Really?" Sheila looks shocked. "But you hate Boston."

True. I'm happy in Salem, with my kitchen and my cats. I don't like to leave town if I can help it. But I also like to be in control, and efficiency is my keyword. If the two of them go, it will be a colossal waste of time. If I go, I might be a little put out, but at least it makes sense.

"It's fine," I tell her, sounding more sure than I feel. I really do hate driving in Boston. "It's not that far. Here." Reaching into my back pocket, I pull out one of the business cards I always carry on me. We have pens all over the kitchen and I scrounge one up. "Give me the address and the name of who I'm supposed to ask for."

Sheila does.

"And it's four cases, right? On our tab?"

"Yup. You can tell Finn that we'll need another four cases next month, too."

I slip my business card back into my pocket. "Let me grab my coat. I should be back in an hour or so. Keep an eye on my muffins."

I REGRET MY OFFER ALMOST IMMEDIATELY. AN HOUR? Try like three, the traffic is so bad.

It isn't until I'm stuck taking a detour around South Boston that I remember the date. March 17th. St. Patrick's Day. The one day of the year that everyone is Irish—and congestion in the city is a bigger nightmare than usual.

What was I thinking? I knew it was getting close to the 17th. Even living in Salem, where we celebrate witches and magic all year long, being a hop, skip, and a jump away from Boston means that I can't spin around without seeing shamrocks, pots of glittering gold, and a hundred different shades of green everywhere. Shit, we spent the last couple of days cranking out loaf after loaf of Irish soda bread for a couple of local bakeries. So, yes, I knew it was getting close to the 17th.

I guess I just didn't realize it was *today*.

It's a good thing that the Irish pub Sheila sent me to isn't in the heart of South Boston; I never would've gotten close to it if it was. As it is, when I finally find Finnegan's, there's nowhere to park. At all. I could try hunting down a parking deck, but that would be ridiculous since it's just me and I'd have to lug four cases of Guinness back to the car.

Huh. Maybe sending the two of them on their own wouldn't have been such a bad idea after all.

Oh, well.

I settle on double-parking in front of the bar, crossing my fingers while praying that I can get in and out before someone notices.

I can say for sure that no one inside of the establishment did. When I step inside the dark pub, I notice that the tables are mainly empty. The long stretch of the bar has a couple of patrons seated along the row, but not many. Probably because it's still early. A television hanging in one corner is airing the St. Patrick's

Day parade that's causing all the detours from the South Side. And, I'm betting, it's where most of the bar goers are currently at.

There's only one guy manning the bar. His head jerks up when he hears the jingling bell over the door as I enter.

He smiles. I stop breathing.

"Welcome to Finnegan's. Kitchen's not open yet, so if you're here for a drink, take a seat at the bar. I'll be with you in a second."

I'm staring. I know I am. Considering I spend most of the little free time I have when I'm not working at home with my two tortoiseshell cats, it's been a while since I've been in a bar. It's been even longer since I've come face to face with a man who makes me lose my head long enough to actually get caught staring.

But this guy?

Oh, boy. He's fucking *gorgeous*. Dark hair, a real deep brown, almost black. Bright green eyes. Those cheekbones. That jaw. His wide shoulders.

And the accent—

The *accent*.

It's musical. Lyrical, even. I'd like to think it was fake, since it's St. Patrick's Day and Finnegan's is an Irish bar, but there's something genuine about it. Most likely the fact that it's not so strong.

Giving my head a clearing shake, I move into the

empty bar. His good looks have got me a little dazzled, not gonna lie, and though I remember exactly why I'm here, that's about all I remember. What was the name of the man I'm looking for?

Once I'm standing across from the Irish Adonis, I reach into my pocket and pull out the business card with the bar's address on it. "Hi. So, um, I'm in a rush— I've double-parked outside and I've got to be going so if you could help me, that would be great. I'm looking for—"

Before I can avoid it, his hand reaches out, rudely snatching the card from my grip. "Finn?" He reads the name written on the card before making it disappear as if by magic. One second, he has it. The next? He hides it in the front pocket of his jeans. "Whatcha lookin' for him for?"

I think about asking for my card back, realize that the daring gleam in his green eyes is waiting for me to so that he can say no, then decide it's not worth it. Instead, folding my hands primly in front of me, I tell him, "He's expecting me."

"Ah, so you don't know. Rush, rush, rush, but you don't know why you're rushin'. Funny thing is, I'm not so sure Finn knows that either seein' as how he's off to Ireland and he didn't mention a stunner like you would be stoppin' by. Pity and a shame. Ah, well, wish I could be more of a help. Sorry."

He turns his back, the slight shake to his shoulders a clue that he's laughing at me. Sorry? Uh. Not quite.

I mean, talk about crappy customer service. Seriously? He's not even giving me the chance to tell him what I've come all this way for.

Ugh. So he's gorgeous and that accent is to die for. Doesn't give him the right to act so la-di-da, above it all. Because, you know what? What's so... so grating is that he obviously *knows* how gorgeous he is, and doesn't even attempt to be a decent human because of it. As if he can be a bastard, and I'll forgive him his cavalier attitude because he's so amazing to look at *and* listen to.

His reaction has me immediately on guard. Rolling my eyes, then shooting daggers at his back, I can't rein in my snippiness. "Yes, because I'm sure the owner of this establishment tells *you* everything."

He turns around, the corner of his mouth quirked up in a knowing grin. "Ah, but you'd be surprised at what the boss tells me. So, you want to fill me in on why you're really here? Besides starin' at me, I mean."

I start to sputter. He caught that, even though I hoped he hadn't. Still, I'm not about to admit that to him. "Excuse me?"

"You're excused, sweetheart. Don't worry. Lookin' is free, but if you want to do more than that? Start by orderin' a couple of drinks." He grabs a bottle, expertly spinning it in the air before catching it by the neck.

"Whiskey's good. I might even share a shot with you if you say please."

Okay. That's it. I didn't come all of this way to be spoken down to like this. He might think he's charming, but if he doesn't give it up? I'm about to grab that bottle out of his hand and crack it over his skull.

"No, thanks. I'd rather go thirsty."

HAPPY ST. PADDY'S

Maddie

HE DIPS HIS HEAD. "TAKES ALL KINDS," HE SAYS BEFORE placing his bottle back on the bar top. With a point, he adds, "The door's back that way since you're not here about our liquor."

"I was," I tell him, huffing. "Make sure to let Finn know that we're grateful for our partnership in the past, but we will no longer be ordering your beer for our catering business."

Right when I'm just about to leave, another guy appears from the back. It hits me that the door was cracked open and he might have heard everything that passed between the bartender and me. Since he looks to be barely on the right side of legal—twenty-one, maybe twenty-two tops—I doubt he has the authority to do anything about his odious co-worker. Then he holds out his hand as if to stop me and I second-guess my first impression.

"Hang on, miss. Are you Sheila? Did you have some fella call earlier about a load of Guinness?"

I resist the urge to stick my tongue out at the other man. At least someone here has half a clue to what's going on.

I'm so eager to get this exchange over with that I don't even bother correcting him. He thinks I'm Sheila? Fine. "Yes. I did."

"Yeah, okay. We've got the four cases you were looking for all wrapped up. You park nearby?"

The Irish man's eyes seem to sparkle. "She says she double-parked out front. Seems she was in a mighty hurry, but didn't know what she was here for. Good thing you know, Jer. Hate to see her get a ticket because she was too busy flirtin' with me to move along."

Is he fucking serious? "You've got to be kidding me—"

The younger man clears his throat. Unlike the dark-haired jerk, he has a name tag on his apron. Jeremy. "If you want to get your car and drive around back, I can load up the beer for you. Get you out of here before the cops flag your car."

The beer. The Guinness. The reason I'm here—and the reason I've had to deal with such an asshole. Good thing the kid popped his head out when he did. I really would've walked out without the damn beer.

Tucking my blonde hair behind my ears, taking a moment to compose myself, I nod. "Thank you. That's really kind of you and I appreciate it. I'll make sure to tell your boss about this." With a sniff, I add, "About both of you."

The tips of Jeremy's ears turn red. I'd think he was an adorable youngster except for the way he's spent the entire conversation talking to my chest. Since he's actually being helpful, I decide to let that go. The other guy? He doesn't have a prayer.

I pull my keys out of my coat pocket, turning toward the entrance.

A chuckle, then a cheery, "Happy St. Paddy's, sweetheart," follows behind me. I don't need to hear the Irish accent to know which man it was.

My hands clench into tight fists at my side. Condescending ass.

Pushing the front door open with my fists, I storm out of the pub, pausing to let loose an angry exhale once I'm a few feet away from the entrance. Why is it that the good looking guys are either taken or gay or complete assholes? No wonder I'm single. I might have been too busy to go out and look for a man lately—not with our business taking up so much of my time—but if that's indicative of what's out there waiting? No thanks. I'll be happy with my two cats.

Another rough exhale and then I shake off the uncomfortable feeling in the pit of my stomach. It bothers me that I let that guy get to me like that. I used to be able to stick up my nose and let cocky bastards like that slide right off my back. There was something about him, though, that really bothered me. Don't know why, only know I didn't care for it at all.

That's it, I decide. Next time Sheila needs Guinness, she can either drive into Boston herself or I'll pick up a can at the nearest Shaw's. I'm not putting up with this BS again.

Just as I'm heading off to move my car, I stop. The early afternoon sun is shining down and it glances off something on the sidewalk in front of me. It winks up at me, the flash nearly blinding. I wince, then cover my eyes with my hand to block the sun before lowering my gaze to look at my feet.

It's... it's a coin. And not a quarter, though it's about the same size. Round and flat, it's a striking gold rather than a dull silver. A face is carved into the side I can see staring up at me. Strangely enough, it's a female face. A queen, maybe? It's definitely foreign.

I reach over and pick it up. Slipping it in my coat pocket, I throw one last dirty look over my shoulder at Finnegan's tinted windows before storming off to find my car.

What a waste of my time. Thank goodness for

Jeremy. I just hope he's quick enough with the beer that I don't get a ticket like that Irish man teased.

Killian

I love this holiday. Not even dealing with Miss Stick-Up-Her-Ass could ruin my good mood today.

It's a shame, too. She's quite a beauty, with that wavy blonde hair and eyes so blue, they remind me of the sky. I thought about putting on the charm for a couple seconds there while she was still smiling, but it was like the sight of me pissed her off. No matter what I did, or how I tried to lighten the mood, she just glared at me as if I was messing around on purpose.

And maybe I was. What's the harm? It's St. Paddy's Day, after all, and if everyone's Irish, the true Irish folk should get a pass. At least, that's what my dad always said. 'Course, he's a full-blooded leprechaun who gets his kicks out of planting rainbows, telling tales, and running his Irish pub. Me? With my human mother's blood mixing with his, I'm only half leprechaun so I mainly run Finnegan's when my dad's not around.

Like today. I love celebrating St. Paddy's in Boston —and, at least, I get to do so. Poor Dad, he has to fly back to Ireland every year for the holiday so that leaves me in charge of Finnegan's until he gets back. Might have been helpful if he told me about the order for the catering lasses before he went, but that's fine. Magic makes him crazy sometimes so I don't blame him. It's one of the reasons I'm glad I'm only half.

Sure, there's a couple of laws I've got to obey. Every leprechaun gets itchy when they see someone else's rainbow, we all have our own pot of gold to guard— mine's hidden in my apartment—and I have this insane urge to wear a red coat. Good thing I'm a Sox fan so there's never a shortage of windbreakers and hoodies. That's about it for me, though.

Well, that and the accent. When I'm tired or stressed or real horny, I sound like the leprechaun I'm supposed to be. Can't help it.

Most of the times, I can control the little bit of magic I have. I've got to. Because one downside to being only half a leprechaun? I've got the worst luck ever. Seriously. I can walk outside, the sky as blue as the day is long, and *boom*. Sudden rainstorm and I'm soaked to my boxers. I've given myself eight black eyes in the last six years and I maybe earned only two of them with my smart mouth. I'm constantly losing my sneakers, but only the left one. It's weird, but I'm used to it, and it could be worse.

I could be in Ireland today, instead of slinging Guinnesses for lovely tourists. And maybe—I slip my hand in my pocket, drawing out the business card I didn't throw away—Ms. Madison Scott wasn't willing to take the stick out of her ass long enough to share a drink with me, but there will be countless others come tonight.

I don't need her, even if my breath quickens a wee bit every time I think of her. I've been walking around with a semi since she strode into Finnegan's like she owned the place. Doesn't even help to remember the disgusted sigh she let out as she stormed out of the pub. In fact, my wayward cock must be into rejection today because it twitches before stiffening a little more.

Giving it a rough stroke with the edge of my palm, tucking it so that it's not so obvious beneath my apron, I slip the business card back into my jeans pocket.

I freeze.

My amulet is missing.

No. No fucking way. I jam my hands in my pocket, fingers probing every corner. Except for Ms. Scott's business card, there's nothing else in there.

How? I don't know how the hell I lost it. For Éire's sake, it's *magic*. I put it in the pocket, it stays there, and it doesn't move until I throw my jeans in the wash and it magically moves to a new pocket. It's done that my entire life. I'm not supposed to be *able* to lose it.

Tell that to my amulet, though. It's habit, when I'm aggravated or I'm anxious or my dad's on my case again, to slip my hand in my pocket and rub the coin-shaped amulet with my thumb. Fiddling with my amulet is also my biggest tell. An old poker buddy of mine pointed it out after the third time he rolled me during our weekly matches. Any time I'm bluffing, I pull my amulet out, flip it between my fingers, then palm it. He got three grand off me before I knew I'd been fleeced.

Since the old poker buddy of mine works as a cupid to make a living, it's not like I could retaliate. The last thing I needed was a pissed off cupid getting revenge on me by shooting me with a love arrow and making me fall for a bar rag or something. I don't know. Henry had a real shifty sense of humor. He might have sworn that I've got too much Faerie blood for the arrow to work. Doesn't mean I believe him.

One thing for sure, though? We're not poker buddies any more, even if he's still a friend of mine. And, okay, I might have a special glass that I save to give him whenever he stops by the bar. And it might not have been washed since that last game, either.

Hey. Three grand is three grand. If I had money like that to blow, I wouldn't have to kill myself working morning, noon, and night at my father's bar. Finnegan's is a a real hole in the wall, a true Irish pub that had the bad luck to be built a couple blocks east of the edge of Southie.

Then again, who am I kidding? With my bad luck, it's a given I'd be stuck behind the bar. What else can I do? It's not like I can actually do anything with my magic. I'm only half, after all. And the half that I am?

Let's just say, I'm not really *that* surprised to find that my amulet isn't where it's supposed to be.

Shite.

"Hey, Kill. You okay? You're looking a little green there, pal."

Jeremy is standing at the other end of the bar, taking inventory on some of the bottles while restocking the others. We might not be in the heart of Southie, but we're going to get a ton of tourists today. There won't be a single pub in Boston that's not packed tonight and it's best to be prepared. So even though he ducked out earlier to help that blonde with the beer, he's back behind the bar, getting ready. It's his second year and he knows what to expect.

Knowing the kid, he's probably walking around, about to go off like a rocket, he's so primed.

St. Paddy's? It's like our Christmas. I'll walk out of here tonight with my wallet bursting with tips and probably a handful of napkins with numbers scrawled on them. The women in town gobble my honest-to-God Irish act up like it's Bailey's Irish Cream. The accent is real—third generation in the States and the part of me that isn't leprechaun just can't shake the brogue—and it's a real panty dropper. I used it to my advantage all throughout my rowdy and reckless early twenties, but now that I'm pushing thirty, I'm a little more choosy about who I go home with.

It's... it's been a while. And maybe I'm feeling pent

up, or maybe it's the sudden realization that my amulet isn't where it's supposed to be. I don't know. My fingers flex and I snap at the poor kid to shut it.

"Sorry, man," Jeremy says, quickly offering an apology while holding up the clipboard like it's a shield. "Didn't mean to piss you off. If you're not feeling too good, I get it. I've been overdoing it myself a little. I got the bar if you want to go sit for a few."

I know he was making a joke. Dad goes a little crazy every year for the holiday and the bar looks like something the Emerald City might've coughed up. There's green everywhere. But as I slip my hand in my pocket, double- and triple-checking that the amulet is mysteriously missing, I feel like I'm about to hurl.

He gave me an excuse. I'm gonna take it.

"You're right. I'm being a dick because my stomach's a wee bit off. Listen, I'm thinking maybe I should head on home. If it starts comin' out one way or the other, you won't want me around."

"But, dude." His jaw actually drops. "The tail!"

I spare him a tiny grin because I was his age once and I probably reacted just the same. Who cares about the business when all you can think about is getting your dick wet, huh?

Shaking my head, I tell him, "Yeah, and half of them I wouldn't bang with your dick even if I was feelin' a hundred percent. It's too easy anyway, boyo.

Don't you like a little chase? It's so much better when you have to work for it."

"You mean like with the blonde earlier?"

My stomach twinges and, despite what I just told Jeremy, it has nothing to do with feeling sick. It's the deep pull of magic, and I really hope it's a coincidence that it hit the second he mentioned the woman from before. Sure, she was super hot, and I meant it when I said I don't mind putting out a little effort, but she shouldn't be able to affect me like this. Especially since I get the idea that she wouldn't give me a second chance even if I did something I'd never do—like begging her to have that drink with me after all.

Of course, I don't admit it. "She'd take some work, ay, and some finessin', but I could have her if I wanted to. She was in a rush, that's all."

"Considering how she was still mumbling under her breath about you when I brought her the beer, you might be right. And, hey, that might be how it is for you, Irish. For us regular folks, we gotta make do with what we can get. If it's easy, that's even better."

I shrug, ignoring the minor twinge at hearing she was still thinking about me after our quick exchange. If what I'm guessing might be true, I'd better hope she's in a better mood the next time we meet.

Which, I'm beginning to suspect, might be sooner than she'd like.

"Whatever you say. Just do me a favor, yeah? If it

ever comes up, don't let Finn know you covered for me. I knock this out, I should be back for the night rush tonight, but in case I can't, maybe call in Mary and Rosalie. Mary's married and Rosalie is dating the hostess from that hipster bistro down the block. No competition for you and your feisty libido."

"Hey, a man's got needs." Then, as if realizing what I said, Jeremy's grin grows wolfish. "How about this: you take care of yourself. Don't even worry about coming in later. I'll just go ahead and give the girls a call."

"And Finn?"

"He won't hear about this from me."

No. He won't.

But if I can't get my amulet back?

The old man will have to hear about it from *me*.

3

IN HER COAT

Maddie

I CALL SHEILA ON MY WAY BACK INTO SALEM. WHEN SHE answers, she's so cheery I almost want to pull over to puke.

"Hey, Maddie! How's Boston?"

"It's St. Patrick's Day. How do you think it is?"

"Oof. Sorry, sweetie. Cole realized that after you left. By then you were probably halfway there so I figured I'd let you find that out for yourself. Was it really that bad? I don't remember Finnegan's being on the South Side."

"It wasn't, but traffic was still ridiculous. I'm only heading back now."

"But you have the Guinness?"

Hmm. No thanks to the dark-haired bartender. "Yeah. I have it."

"Thank you, thank you, Maddie! Things have been so hectic, with the new kitchen, and Cole moving into my place. I still don't know how I let that slip my mind. Don't worry. It won't happen again."

It won't, and not only because Sheila is normally way too organized to let something like this happen a second time. Next time we're getting low, I'll make sure to point it out to Sheila myself. Let her take the drive into Boston and hope the owner is there. I don't ever want to see that smarmy Irish bastard again.

"I know. It's fine." The light ahead of me turns red and I coast up to the box. I don't know why, but I'm tired. Really tired. Yawning as I lay my head back against the headrest, I say, "I'm going to stop in and drop the beer off, then I think I'm done for the day. I'm beat."

"Sure thing, sweetie. My bread is just about done and Cole finished baking the last of your muffin batter before getting a lot of the chopping done for tomorrow. We'll stick it out until you get back so that we can help you unload the beer from your car. Those cases are fucking heavy. Last time I had to lug them into my house all by myself."

Of course, she did; the Guinness bread is her specialty. Besides, I know my own strengths and weaknesses. Actual physical strength? Yeah, that's definitely a weak point for me. I like to think I'm normal: normal height, normal weight, normal looks. Pretty average all around. But when my business partner is a fucking Amazon woman? And her boyfriend is just as tall and incredibly muscular? I'll let them carry the Guinness in for me.

I hear a muffled voice. Sheila laughs at whatever Cole must have said before hushing him and telling him to go check on her sourdough.

Once he's far enough away, she laughs again. "Cole says he'll unload the beer by himself so that I don't have to. Please. Just because we're shacking up, it doesn't mean I'm suddenly some helpless damsel in distress. I can carry a case of beer into the fridge without him holding my hand."

"I don't know, Sheil, maybe you should let him. You know how fragile male egos can be sometimes."

Another chuckle. "Trust me, sweetie, Cole prefers it when I take charge. It really gets him going, if you know what I mean."

Considering how often I find the two of them necking in the kitchen after Sheila gives him an order or tells him what to do, I think I get it. My nose wrinkles. "Too much info. Thanks for that."

"Any time. See you in a few?"

"Yeah. Bye."

Pressing the button on my steering wheel, I kill the connection to my hands-free call, then slip my hand into my coat pocket. I keep mints in there and I'm reaching for one when my fingers brush against something cool, something smooth.

And I remember: the coin.

I squeeze the coin for a second, thinking about how happy Sheila sounds. Cole's perfect for her, and not just because he got us the new headquarters for S&M as some grand gesture of his love. She's not wrong. With her explosive personality and tendency to overdo it, she needed someone who was strong enough to love her and smart enough not to try to rein her in. From everything I've seen so far, Cole is just the guy.

I want that.

Closing my eyes, exhaling softly through my nose, I think to myself: *I wish I had someone who loves me like that*. And then, because I know my girls are devoted to me, I have to add: *A human person. A man.*

I want a man of my own to love.

A horn screeches behind me. My eyes spring open and, look at that, some more green. Only it's not the garish decorations I left behind at Finnegan's, but the vibrant green on the swaying traffic light. Green means go.

I go.

Because most of the traffic is due to tourists trying to get *into* Boston, the drive back to Salem is a lot smoother than I expect. Within an hour, I've stopped at the new S&M headquarters, watched as Cole and

Sheila argued over who was going to bring the Guinness inside, waited as each carried in two cases, then drove home. By the time I had parked in my driveway, it was almost seven o'clock and it was just starting to get dark.

I yawn again, cursing Daylight Savings. That has to be why I'm feeling so drained. Losing that hour always seems to affect me way worse than gaining one. Plus, now my girls' schedule is all off. The second I let myself into my house, both Daisy and Stewie—and, yes, they're both girls despite Stew's name—are at my feet, mewling at my ankles. They want their wet food and they want it *now*.

"Okay, okay. I'm coming, ladies. Give Mama a second and I'll get dinner ready," I coo, dropping my purse on the couch before heading straight into the kitchen. I don't even bother taking my coat off. Kitties first. Comfort second.

I break open a can of Fancy Feast and divide it into their matching bowls. I thought it was cute, getting them the same small pink bowl, since they're basically twins. I can tell them apart—Daisy has a white tip on her tail that Stewie doesn't have—but to anyone else, they're too close to differentiate at first glance.

I reach down, giving each girl a scratch between her ears while they scarf up their wet food. Jeez, you'd think I starve them. Shaking my head, I straighten and head back to my dining room. I need to get started on my own dinner but, first, I want to sit down and see if I can get a few pieces done on my most recent puzzle.

I... I *love* puzzles. Getting them organized, finding the pieces, the satisfaction of an exact fit... it's the perfect stress reliever for me. I'm in the middle of a monstrous ten thousand piece puzzle featuring—what else—a group of cats playing outside in a garden. I'm maybe a third of the way done. I've got the edges complete, and all of the different color groups set together, plus a few big chunks already assembled. Because of the new kitchen, I've been too busy to work on it the way that I usually do. Since I'm home earlier than usual, I'm looking forward to it.

It's taken me a very long time to train my girls not to bother any of my puzzles in progress. Now I can leave them on the dining room table, knowing that they'll be in one piece when I return. A quick check to make sure it hasn't been disturbed—it hasn't—and then I decide I'd rather work on my puzzle while Daisy and Stew are eating. I can grab some food later.

Just as I'm about to take my coat off and take a seat, I hear my doorbell ring.

That's odd. I wonder who that could be?

Even though I live alone in a nice neighborhood, I'm still cautious. Instead of opening the door, I peek out through my window first, then head for the door when it seems like a harmless dark-haired man is standing patiently on my porch. I didn't really get a good look at his face since he had his head turned as he glanced behind him toward the street, but he doesn't look like an axe murderer or anything.

Grabbing my cell phone from my purse just in case, I open the door.

"Hi. Can I help— wait a sec... I know you! You're the guy from the bar!"

"Aye. And you're the sticky-fingered lass who walked off my amulet."

There's something different about him and when it takes me a second to understand exactly what he means, I realize it's his accent. What was a hint of Irish back when I met him at Finnegan's is now a full-blown, over the top brogue. Wonderful. It's so thick, I barely understand him.

I understood him plenty back at Finnegan's. Now? Not even close. I've always had a hard time picking up really strong accents. I even watch television with the closed captions on because it's too difficult for me sometimes.

My mom always said it's because my mind is going a mile a minute and I never take the time to focus. I force myself to try. A second later, my jaw is just about on my floor.

"Are you accusing me of taking something of yours? Of *stealing* your... your amulet?"

"It's what I said, isn't it?"

With a sniff, I compose myself enough to snap, "I don't steal."

"Maybe not on purpose, but you have it. Trust me on this." When it's clear I'm not budging, he sighs. "It's round, about the size of a quarter, but a nice, shiny gold."

I don't steal. I *don't*. I also try to be as honest as possible. A little white lie, sure, what's the harm in one of those? Denying that his... his amulet thing isn't in my pocket right now? I can't do it. I just can't.

And he knows it.

He smirks. And, damn it, I really want to hate that smirk. I didn't think it was possible, but it makes him even more attractive.

Grr.

Killian

Ms. Madison Scott is growling at me. I don't even know if she realizes she's doing it.

It's fucking adorable.

But that doesn't stop me from insisting. "You have it. I know you do."

She can deny it as much as she likes. The second she opened the door, it's like a one-two punch. She's even prettier than I remember, and the screwed up expression of bafflement she wears is so absolutely cute that I can almost forgive it when it turns into a noticeable scowl. As if my bad luck can't get any worse, my body immediately begins to react to being this close to her again. This woman is a thief and she glares at me like I'm a worm. Less than a worm. I shouldn't want her as bad as I do.

And that's not all. The magic that's kept my insides twisted all the way from Boston to Salem slams right into my chest the instant I see her again. It's my amulet. She definitely has it.

I take a deep breath, searching for the source of it. I already know it's coming from this woman. With a little bit of concentration, I zero in on her left-hand side. Her coat pocket.

"Check your coat."

I don't point at which side on purpose. When her left hand goes right to that pocket, I let my lips quirk upward. I knew I was right.

She doesn't take it out, though. Hands on her hips now, she narrows her gaze on me.

"Did you come all the way here to accuse me of stealing something I *found*? How was I supposed to know it was yours?" And then, as if just realizing something, she outright glares up at me, suspicion written in her pale blue eyes. "How *did* you know how to find me? Oh, jeez. The business card. I gave you my business card."

"What? This?" Even though she still hasn't taken my amulet back out yet, I'm kind enough to retrieve that business card I still haven't been able to get rid of. "How did this help me find you?"

"My address— oh. This is my new card, with the new address on it."

"Exactly." I tuck the card away again before she can snatch it back.

"Then how did you find me? Did you... did you follow me here?"

"What? Please. Don't flatter yourself, sweetheart. It wasn't my choice, believe me. No. I followed the magic."

She blinks. "The magic?"

I nod. It's clear that she's as human as my mom is so she definitely doesn't know anything about magic. And I don't really think she took my amulet on purpose. Doesn't change the truth, though—she has it, and she's going to have to deal with the consequences of her actions. Even as a half leprechaun, I have to abide by the rules.

And having a wee mortal female find my amulet? That's one of the biggies.

There's no way to explain what I mean. I don't even waste my breath trying. I could tell her I'm a half-blood leprechaun and she could threaten me with the men in the white coats. No thanks. Never a good start to a real relationship if one of the couple thinks the other is looney tunes.

And... now I'm hoping for a relationship with this amulet thief.

Shite.

I'm all messed up. No wonder Dad always warned me against letting anything happen to my amulet. I need to get it back.

I need to go.

4

KILLIAN'S A SNACK

Killian

FIRST THINGS FIRST. I CAN'T GO ANYWHERE WITHOUT MY amulet—and there's only one way to get it back.

I've got a feeling this isn't gonna end well, but I've got to try. Calling up my most charming smile, I ask, "Can I come inside?"

Suddenly, there's an arm stretched across the door, blocking me from moving any closer.

"I don't think that's a good idea," Madison adds unnecessarily.

She's probably right. Still, it's not like I can do what I'm about to do outside. Now that she's involved in the geis, it's within my rights to show her exactly what kind of Faerie she's dealing with. If anyone else finds out that I'm part leprechaun, there could be trouble. I have to get inside.

Leprechauns are tricky. It's one of our best qualities. And because I'm the unlucky schmuck who can barely tap into my magic, I'm really rotten when it comes to being deceptive. The most I can do is point over her shoulder and say, "What's that?"

I'm guessing Madison is as bad at trickery as I am. Just like I expect, her head spins, long blonde hair fanning out as she looks behind her.

Grabbing her by the shoulders, I ease her to the side. She's a wee thing, barely coming up to my chin, and I move her far enough from the door to allow me to slip inside.

I have the door shut smartly behind me before she starts shouting.

"What are you— get the fuck out of here!" She lifts her hand up, brandishing a cell phone I hadn't noticed before. "I'm giving you to the count of three and then I'm calling the cops."

She'll do it, too. I can see the gleam in her eyes, the way her lips go thin. She's not bluffing.

Great. Cops are the last complication I want or need.

Holding up my hands, attempting to placate her, I say, "Listen, I had to do it. You don't want your neighbors gettin' involved."

"*I* don't want to get involved. And that's one."

Here goes nothing. "It's about the magic. Listen, I know you won't get it, but I'm a leprechaun, alright? And you stealin' my amulet has consequences."

"I didn't steal anything, there's no such things as leprechauns, and you're not funny. St. Patrick's Day is almost over and you're going to spend the rest of it in a fucking cell. Two."

Once again, she's reacting just the way I figured she would. Ah, well. Sometimes the old ways are the best. Seeing is believing.

"Thr—"

It's been years since I've done this. It used to be a party trick I pulled all the time when I hung around other people like me. The mythical creatures. The magical. The fantastical. I might've left most of that life behind me when I gave up on my heritage, but there's still a few tricks I do have up my sleeve.

She never finishes her threat. Before she can spit out the last part of *three*, I go from being my full height of 6'3" down to a mere six inches high.

Full-blooded leprechauns have a much wider ranger. My dad can be three inches to seven feet tall and everything between. Me? I'm either half a foot or my real height. That's it. It's all I need, really. The second I'm staring at her shin before tilting my head back to see the dazed look of surprise on her face, I know I've got her right where I want her.

No way she can explain away this without resorting to magic. Because it *is* magic. I am part-leprechaun.

And I'm about to be a snack.

It all happens so fast. I want to keep this size for a few moments, give her time to adjust to exactly what she's seeing. If I change back too quickly, she can pretend to have imagined it. I need her to accept it. Except, within seconds, the air is split by a high-pitched yowling sound and, out of nowhere, a giant furry beast comes charging at me.

It's a cat. The logical man-brain inside of my head knows that. Try telling that to the six-inch high magical creature whose primal instincts remember what it was like to be hunted by saber-tooth tigers.

It's either it or me, and considering I have nothing to defend myself with while I'm mini-Killian, my only choice is to grow back to my normal height again.

Just as the cat swipes at me, I find the magic deep inside and give it a tug.

Suddenly, I'm the right size again. I tower over the cat. It hisses and bats at my boot before fluffing up like the furball it is. It realizes in an instant that I'm no longer the easy prey I was a few seconds ago. Spooked and much smarter than I would've given it credit for, the cat's claws scrabble at the wooden floor as it wheels around and retreats, disappearing into the hallway.

I try not to let Madison see how close of a call that was. Readjusting my hooded sweatshirt, taking a second to calm my racing heart, I brush my hair out of my eyes and glance over at her.

She's gaping at me.

Well, that's better than calling the cops, I guess.

Maddie

He's a leprechaun.

I—

I—

Holy shit.

I'm glad now that he tricked his way inside of my house. I don't know what I would've done if he shrunk down like that on my front porch. It would've bad enough if my neighbors saw that, but I don't think my first reaction would've been to slam the door in his face. Punting him with the tip of my sneaker might've been more my style once I got past my shock.

At least that would've been a better fate than what Daisy had in store for him. Not that I can blame my girl. As small as he was, he looked like vermin. Of course she was going to come check him out. She might be a little chunky, and definitely spoiled, but Daisy is a stray I rescued when I first moved out on my own and the old girl is still a mouser at heart.

Only the bartender from Finnegan's isn't a mouse.

He's a fucking leprechaun.

Calm down, Maddie. So he's a leprechaun. It

could've been worse. At least, when he shrunk down to a miniature size, his clothes shrunk with him so I didn't have a six inch tall leprechaun streaking across my living room—

Wait. What am I thinking? How is that a good thing? Because he might be a leprechaun, not to mention a bit of a cocky asshole, but he's still the best looking guy I've seen in ages. Seriously. You would think his magic show would make him less attractive. Nope. Even his personality isn't enough to stop me from gobbling him up with my eyes.

I watch as he glares down the hall where Daisy made her escape, his green eyes wide and a little spooked. I can hear how fast he's breathing for a second before he visibly calms down. Turning away from me, he tugs on his sleeve, adjusting his sweatshirt now that he's big again.

It's a Boston Red Sox sweatshirt, which strikes me as a little weird since it's St. Patrick's Day and I would've guessed a leprechaun would be decked out in green. He is from Boston, though, and he's also a guy. Who knows? Maybe his loyalty to his team is more important to him than fulfilling a stereotype.

And, oh my god, here I am, trying to make some kind of logical sense out of this. What is *wrong* with me?

Though, I have to admit, with the luck of the Irish on their side, maybe that's why they've become such a good team lately. I'm not the biggest baseball fan, but when the Sox won the World Series last year, all of Massachusetts seemed to shake. With a record like theirs, suspecting a little magic help wouldn't be too far fetched of an idea.

Because magic is real. Leprechauns are real.

Holy crap.

As I'm struggling to accept what I just discovered—and no doubt about it, his shrinking act was very convincing—the leprechaun messes with his hair, running his hands through the length before resettling the way the big red hood of his sweatshirt falls down his back.

"You could've warned me you had those wee furry monsters, sweetheart. Beasts with claws, they are. Shite."

His thick accent—and this time I'm sure of it, it's even thicker than before—rips me out of my stupor.

"Yeah," I shoot back, "well, you could've warned me you were going to do that, you... you *leprechaun*!"

"Half, actually. My dad's full-blooded but my mother's as human as you are." He shrugs. "Just thought I'd mention that. And, to be fair, I did try to warn you. You weren't havin' it."

He's got a point. I *hate* that he's got a point.

"Ugh!"

Sudden concern flashes across his face, the honest expression making him even more handsome. He reaches his hand out, settling it on the shoulder of my coat. Because I'm still wearing my coat, with the stupid gold coin that got me into this mess hidden away in my pocket.

"How are you doin'? Good? Some people don't do so well with the truth. You need to sit down?"

"I'm fine," I snap, shaking him off. I mean it, too. I'll probably have a total breakdown later, when I'm in the sanctity of my room and I don't have to see that... that goddamn smirk of his; it might not be there now, but it'll be back, I know it. Until then, I'll deal. He's a leprechaun? Fine. No denying what my own two eyes just showed me. Especially since my Daisy nearly *ate* him.

Crap, maybe I should ask him if *he* needs a seat. No. Better not. The way he tried to recover after the scare tells me it affected him more than he wanted me to know; there's that whole "fragile male ego" thing again. Not to mention, if I give him a seat, he might think I'm inviting him to stay.

And I'm not. This freaky leprechaun guy has got to go.

Besides, I'm still focusing on the whole "you stole my coin" thing. To me, that's the real issue here. My integrity is way more important than my sanity right now, and I'm not so sure what that says about me, but I don't care.

Pulling the golden coin out of my pocket, I lift it up

so that he can see it. "I really didn't take your coin. I found it outside your pub."

His eyes light up, as if he thinks this is funny. I'm glad one of us does.

"Potato, Pot-ah-to. Either way, you've got it now."

Not anymore. I thrust it out at him. "Here you go. Take it."

"I wish I could, but it's not so easy as you just handin' it back to me, sweetheart. Fact is, you've got it, and the magic says I can't leave until you get three wishes."

More Magic? Wishes? If it wasn't for what I just saw with my own two eyes, I would think he had lost it. Maybe I'm the one who has since I can't stop myself from saying, "You mean like a genie?"

He scoffs. Jeez, how can he make a *scoff* attractive? "Be glad I'm not a genie. They love to twist the wishes up. Me, I just want to grant them and be on my way. I've got the St. Paddy's rush at the bar to deal with tonight, and I don't trust leavin' Jer alone, so let's get the show on the road. Come on. Three wishes. That's all it takes. You make 'em, I get my coin back, we're done. Let's go."

Okay. Fine. If that's all it takes to make this weirdo happy, fine. He has to know what he's talking about, right? And even if he's messing with me, he's got to figure out the wish thing. Good luck.

Just in case, I make sure to ask, "I can wish for anything?"

"Nothing crazy, I'm hopin'. I've really got to be leavin'."

"Okay. Three wishes and you're gone." And then I can sit down with Daisy and Stewie and lose my shit in peace. "Fine." Wait—what do I wish for? I glance over at him, the way his arms are stretched across his red sweatshirt, the way his legs are braced wide, unmoving. And the words pop out, "Um... I wish for a banana."

"A banana? Really?"

The way he drawls that somewhere over my head makes me realize that my eyes are still lingering on his jeans. And, oh my god, I can't believe I actually said that. My whole face flushes, like my cheeks are on fire. I'm stubborn enough to pretend that I don't notice.

"What's wrong with a banana?" I ask, daring to meet the twinkle in his bright green eyes. "Potassium is good for you. And you're the one who said to keep it simple."

"You're right. It's fine, they're your wishes anyway. Anything to get my amulet back. One banana, coming up." He holds out his hand. "Ripe or green?"

"What? Does it matter?"

"Let's go green. It is the holiday, after all." He glances at his hand. His *empty* hand. "Say, you don't see a banana, do you?"

There's something about the light-hearted way he says that. I can already tell that he is a tease, but that's a little bit *too* light-hearted. "No banana," I confirm.

His face suddenly shadows, going impossibly dark. Something's really wrong. "You... you didn't make any wishes before I got here, did you?"

"What? No. Of course not. Why would I be making wishes?"

"Don't rightly know, but there's no banana. That's why I said don't make 'em crazy. My magic's not strong enough to take care of more than one wish at a time. Remember? Half-blood? So, for me, it's one, then another, then the last. No banana? That means I'm already workin' on a wish."

"But I didn't make any wish!"

"Magic says otherwise. And I can't get my amulet back until the three wishes are done. Ain't you the lucky one. Looks like you just got yourself a roommate."

A roommate? Oh, no. No, no, no. No fucking way.

"You're not staying here. In fact, you have to leave now. Go."

"No can do, sweetheart. See, you've got something of mine. I told you about the wishes, yeah? It's a leprechaun thing. By the way, since we're gonna be roomies a while, might as well tell you my name. It's Killian. Killian Finnegan."

I'm just about to snap that I couldn't care less what

his name was when it hits me. Finnegan. Like the bar. "Finnegan?" I echo.

He nods. "Finn's my dad. And, yeah, he's a leprechaun, too. And I'd like to get this straightened out as quickly as possible, if you don't mind. He's in Ireland for the next couple of weeks, but I'm in for one hell of an *I told you so* if I don't have my amulet back before then."

"Amulet?"

"The coin. Same thing. Either way, it's mine and I won't be leavin' until I've got it back in my possession."

Reaching behind him, he lifts the hem of his Red Sox hoodie up and over his head, mussing his already tousled dark hair. He runs his hand through it again, fixing it a bit, before folding up his sweatshirt and tossing it on my nearby couch.

It looks like he's getting ready to make himself at home here. In *my* home.

Hell, no. He wants a wish? I'll make a wish!

"I wish you would just go away!"

"Yeah, well, I wish you hadn't walked off with my amulet. Now, tell me, which room is the one you'll be lettin' me have?"

5

DEFINITELY NOT GEESE

Maddie

"I'M SORRY—WHAT?"

"My room. Until I can get my amulet back, I'm gonna stay right here."

I live alone. Apart from Daisy and Stewie, it's just me. Sure, I have two rooms because that's how my house is built, but that doesn't mean I'm about to let a stranger stay in my house because he's insisting that is his plan. Who does he think he is? I don't care if he's St. Patrick himself, there's no way I'm inviting him to stay over in my house because I had the really crappy luck to pick up his stupid coin.

"No." I shake my head so sternly, I nearly pull a muscle. "You can't."

"Aye, but I can. I have to. That's the magic, sweetheart. You took my coin, you get my wishes. It's how it works. I can't change it. Neither can you."

"Okay, first of all? The name's Madison, okay? Not sweetheart. Second? I didn't *take* your stupid coin, I *found* it. Here." I dig the coin out of my pocket again, reaching out and pressing it against the inside of his hand. "I told you before. Take it back. I don't want any stupid wishes anyway."

"You think it's that simple?"

It should be. It *has* to be. "Yes."

"Really?" Killian holds his hand up, revealing an empty palm. No banana, no old coin. "Then where's my amulet, *Madison*?"

"I—"

He scoffs. "Check your pocket."

"How would it have gotten there?" I demand. He didn't move. As much as I'm trying not to stare, I haven't be able to take my eyes off of this guy since he knocked on my door. I would've seen him if he slipped it in my pocket. *He didn't move.*

"Humor me. Just go on and check it."

I do. The second my fingers dip inside my pocket, the tips brushing against the engraved metal of the coin, I feel my stomach sink. What the hell? I pull it out, just to make sure. "How did you do that? That's not funny. Practice your magic tricks on someone else. Take this." I hold the coin out to him again. "Take the stupid fucking thing and go."

"You've got a mouth on you, you know."

"Your point? Just because I'm blonde and a chick, doesn't mean I can't use a perfectly valid word to show you how fucking crazy you're making me. Now go. I'm not kidding."

He backs up, crossing his arms over his wide chest. I try not to notice how the sleeves of his Finnegan's polo shirt are almost strangling his massive biceps. Why does he have to look so good and act like such an ass? I'm done with his games. And that's what they are. Games.

I don't know what I did—okay. No. I *do* know what I did: I picked up a stupid, shiny coin. Sue me. I thought it was a souvenir. Like a rational human being, it never occurred to me that it might be a leprechaun's magic coin. And now *I* have to pay for it?

Because I can tell. My older brother Silas is the same. The second I saw the set of his jaw, I was sunk. Killian isn't going to leave until he's good and ready, and nothing short of calling the police like I first threatened and having them drag his big, muscular body out of my house is going to get rid of him.

And how will that even work? He's magic! Daisy almost ate him, for god's sake, because he managed to shrink down to almost nothing before returning to the gorgeous man in front of me.

I have so many questions. *So* many questions. Like, if his stupid amulet thing is so important, how did I find it outside? What does he mean when he says that it's magic, and that the magic enabled him to follow me from Boston all the way to Salem? If he's supposed to be able to grant my wishes, where is my banana? Not that I really wanted one, but still. He said make a wish. I did.

And now he thinks he's going to stay here? With *me*?

Hell no. Uh-uh. Nope.

I might have to believe he's a mythical creature. With the thick Irish brogue and how he shrunk like that, he's definitely a leprechaun. I might understand the lengths he's going to maintain this crazy idea that he owes me something if I stumbled upon his pot of gold maybe. But this one coin?

I... I just don't understand.

With a sigh, I ask, "What's so important anyway? Is it just because it's gold?"

Killian clutches his chest, like I gave him a heart attack. He actually pales. "Just gold? Gold is never *just gold*, woman."

Overdramatic drama queen. I'm the one who has been surprised by a stubborn leprechaun—sorry, *half* leprechaun—in my home. Maybe he's teasing, too. I don't know, but I'm not about to let this go.

"Why is it magic?" Because there's no denying that, either. "Why can't I give it back?"

"I told you. It's the geis—"

This is getting ridiculous. "Now there's *geese* involved."

"No. Geis. G-E-I-S. It's like a promise. The amulet is a sign of my promise. I get the magic—as much as I can, being half—and the amulet is... it's hard to explain to you humans. I'm just supposed to have it and it's really bad if I don't. I can't be me without it, and it gives you power over me. That's why you get your wishes. It's your reward for returning it to me."

"But I don't want any reward! I just want you to take the stupid thing and leave me alone!"

"Magic don't care, sweetheart."

He's really pushing his luck. If I'm being honest, I'm probably holding on by a thread. Every time he says *sweetheart* is another fray snapping away from the line. It took me half of high school to get used to Sheila calling me *sweetie*. Every *sweetheart* grates on my nerve until that last one makes me growl.

I actually *growl*. Forget cursing. He's reduced me to making animal sounds!

"Sorry," he shrugs. "Magic don't care, Maddie."

You've got to be kidding. *Maddie*'s even worse than *sweetheart*!

"It's Madison!" I shoot back. "Madison, okay? Only my friends get to call me Maddie."

He has the audacity to shrug. "Dependin' on how long it takes before we can get this sorted out, we might get to know each other pretty well. Might as well

53

get used to it." He pauses, the corner of his mouth twitching just a little. "Maddie."

Okay. That's it.

I throw my hands up in the air and walk away from him. Let him sleep outside in his car, I don't care. So I can't call the cops. They'd probably put me away at North Shore for seeing little green men if they even took it seriously. It's St. Patrick's Day, after all. They'd probably think it was a prank.

I really wish it was.

Killian

When Madison storms away, going deeper into the house, I take that as an invitation. What else can I do? I wasn't kidding when I said I was going to be her new roommate. After how the magic compelled me all the way from Boston to Salem, I know that walking away from her while she still has my amulet is impossible.

She'll figure that out eventually. I might not have been able to explain it all that well, but she'll learn. There's no fighting the magic. Until I can get my luck working on the right side for once—yeah, right—I won't be leaving any time soon. Wishes will work eventually. I just gotta bide my time for now.

Too bad my dad is on vacation. He'd eat this up. All my life, he's been after me to embrace my leprechaun side. Easy for him to say, considering he's fullblood and a whizz with the magic. As much as I love my mom, she's pure human. Sometimes the magic wins out, sometimes the human is in charge. Except for my accent, my amulet, and the parlor trick that nearly got me eaten, I'm basically my mother's son. Falling under the geis to grant Madison three wishes is the most leprechaun-y I've ever been. He'd absolutely love it.

Actually, now that I'm thinking about it, I probably should tell him. At least, after he laughed at my predicament, he might be able to help me figure out how to fix this.

I don't know why I thought I'd actually make it back to Finnegan's tonight. It's not like I've ever had any luck. It was obvious in retrospect that it wouldn't be so easy as having her make her wishes. Whether it's my half status or the way I've never been able to get a handle on the Faerie magic, your guess is as good as mine, but this whole day's been a major screw-up since the moment my amulet vanished.

My phone is in the back pocket of my jeans. Pulling it out, I check the screen. It's dead. Of course, it is. Technology and magic don't mix. The second I tapped into my leprechaun side to show off, my phone would've shorted out.

I follow after her.

"Hey. Since I'm going to be staying here—"

She's halfway down the hall when she turns to cut me off. "You're not."

I ignore that. "—do you think you can let me borrow your phone? I have to make a call real quick."

Madison narrows her gaze. She gets the cutest little wrinkle in between her eyebrows as she glares. "Is it local?"

Finn's in Ireland, but I'm not about to tell her that he's the one I'm calling. "Local enough."

"Mm." She pauses for a moment, then lets out a resigned sigh. I have a feeling I'm going to have to get used to those. She looks like the *sigh*-ing type. "Come with me."

She leads me into the biggest, cleanest kitchen I've seen in a small two-story house. I gape at the contraptions lining up neatly along the nearest counter before noticing the wall Madison walked over to.

Good lord, the woman has a landline.

Apart from Finnegan's business line, I haven't used an old-fashioned handset in ages. It's not even a cordless. How fucking quaint. At least it's modern enough that it's not a rotary or I'd take forever trying to turn all the numbers it takes to connect to Ireland.

When I finally do, ignoring Madison's pointed stare when she realizes I fibbed, I put the phone to my ear and wait as it rings and rings. Dad doesn't answer the phone.

I'm not surprised. Ireland is four hours ahead of Massachusetts so now that's is almost 7:15 here, it's after eleven across the Atlantic. St. Paddy's will be winding down. Knowing my dad, Finn will either be out celebrating still or crashed out on my granny's couch with Mom standing over him, shaking her head at how much he overdoes it every year. I won't hear from him until tomorrow morning at the earliest. And it's pointless to try to reach Mom because, as a human, she can't help me with the magic; as my mom, she'll only worry that my bad luck is acting up again.

Which it obviously is.

Shite. Why can't things go right for me just once?

After the phone seems to ring for an eternity, the voicemail comes on. I leave a brief message, telling my father that the bar's in good hands even if the status of my amulet is iffy. Then, if he wants to find out more, he can call me back at this number because this is where I'll be until I get everything straightened out with my magic. And, hey, if he has any advice, I'm all ears.

I hang up, immediately aware that Madison isn't glaring at me anymore. Is it crazy that I miss that?

Perhaps.

Where did she go?

It takes me a second. She's a wee thing, more than a head shorter than me, and she fits so snugly underneath her cozy kitchen table that I don't notice her at first. It isn't until I hear the soft clicking of her tongue, followed by a gentle coo-ing sound, that I find her. She's on her knees, long blonde wavy hair falling in front of her as she extends her hand out, scratching the head of—

My hands go to my hips. I don't know whether to be annoyed or amused and settle on huffing just loud enough to catch her attention.

"What are you doin', Maddie? Checking up on your foul beastie?"

I kept my voice light. She still jumps, nearly whacking her head on the top of the table, before glaring up at me from between the legs of the chair nearest her. The cat reacts as well, letting out a sharp *hiss* before she darts out of the kitchen.

"You scared her!"

Am I supposed to feel bad about that? "She was gonna eat me!"

"Yeah, well, that would've been a tragedy." Backing out from under the table, Madison wipes her hands on her pants before rising up to her feet. Then, mimicking my stance, jutting her chin out just so as she tilts her head back so that she can meet my eyes, she dares me to reply.

But I can't. I guess you could say cat's got my tongue because I'm temporarily speechless. She's a feisty one. Oh, Lord, I love the feisty ones.

It's got everything to do with my unlucky streak. If it comes too easy, it's suspicious. Good things never last so, after a while, I stopped looking toward the future, preferring to live in the here and now. I'm used to things never going my way. If I work hard for them, at least I earned them. And if I want something bad enough and can't have it, well, that's just my luck.

Trouble is, the amulet might have brought me back to face off against Madison Scott, but if I managed to get it right back? I might've still been trying to find a way to stay. The more she fights me on this, the more I can't stop myself from wondering what she'd be like once I got past her prickly outer shell. I got a hint of the fire when she snapped at me for calling her Maddie—which is why I'll keep on doing it. Why not, right? That spark might be the closest I get to seeing what makes her burn.

It's my turn to sigh. What a shame. "You really don't like me, do you?"

6

NEON GREEN

Killian

A HINT OF REMORSE FILLS HER BIG, BABY BLUES. "IT'S not that. Listen, Killian, I'm sure you're a fine... um, leprechaun-man-person. Whatever. And maybe we got off on the wrong foot at your father's bar—"

"Aye, when I was bein' my charmin' self?"

"You might've been going for charming," she says, "but it came off as cocky. Anyway, it doesn't matter. This is weird— you gotta admit this is really weird."

She's not wrong. I've been living with the Faerie magic my whole life so I *know* this is weird. I shouldn't have been able to misplace my amulet—and I did. Leprechaun lore is pretty clear on what happens when a human does get their grubby hands on one of our amulets, but I wasn't even able to grant one simple wish, let alone three.

So it's weird, but that doesn't change anything. Until the amulet is back in my pocket where it belongs, this is where I'm going to be staying—and as much as she might think it's my choice, it isn't.

It's like how I had to go leprechaun to prove myself to her. Nothing less than seeing the truth for herself is going to convince this one.

Luckily, it's pretty mild for March. I barely feel the slight chill as I walk back outside. I purposely left my Sox hoodie on the couch because I have no intention of leaving Madison Scott's home just yet. First, though, I have to show her why it's impossible for me to go.

By the time I've hopped down from her porch, moving down the driveway, I hear Madison's hesitant steps follow shortly behind me.

"Where are you going? Isn't that your car right there?"

It is. I parked my car in the drive right behind hers. Ignoring her question, I walk right on by it. Driving's out of the question right now, even if I will have to return to my car to retrieve my duffel bag from the trunk. I'd been hoping it wouldn't be necessary, but I'm used to my lifelong run of being unlucky. Things rarely work out for me. Getting my amulet back without any problems? Deep down, I knew better than to wish for that.

So I packed up a couple of outfits and a few odds and ends I thought—or hoped—I'd need. Considering how bad off I was while I was throwing everything into my duffel, I figured I would have to stay somewhere nearby for at least the night. Now that I'm here, especially now that the wishes aren't working, I'm not banking on being back in Boston any time soon.

I keep walking. The cramps start when I'm about four houses down from hers. A couple more steps and the dull aches become sharp, shooting pains that make me hunch over. It's like trying to push through a brick wall, each step taking a monumental amount of effort. Sweat breaks out along my hairline.

I breathe through my nose, clenching my jaw tight to keep my dinner from coming back up.

Fucking magic. This is even worse than before. At least the nausea wore off once I gave in to the compulsion and left my house, driving toward Salem—driving toward Madison. By the time her house was in my sights, the magic sickness was a bitter memory. I never wanted to feel that again, but if this is how I get her to stop fighting me on this? Fine. I can take it.

Maybe not. The sickness returns with a fucking vengeance. I struggle for two more feet before it brings me to my knees.

A gasp, and the whisper of my name in her noticeable accent. The sounds of sneakered feet slapping against the sidewalk.

As soon as she's about ten feet away from me, the pain mellows and the queasiness begins to fade. It's all but gone by the time she's hovering behind me. Madison ran to my side when I fell, stopping just out of reach as if afraid I'm going to turn around and hurl on her sneakers or something. And you know what? A few seconds ago I might have.

I can be a prick. I accepted that a long, long time ago. Once my guts feel like they've settled back into place, I turn my head to the side, glancing up at her horrified expression.

With a shaky grin, I say, "You saw what happens when I get too far away from my amulet. Not sure about you, but it might be pushin' it to have me sleep in my car or even on your couch. So, about that room..."

Maddie

I sleep like garbage all night. Wouldn't you? I've got a stranger in the guest room down the hall from mine and only his word that he's not some crazy psycho.

Okay. So he's a leprechaun. His magic trick with the shrinking proves that. And, unless he's an amazing actor, he definitely gets violently ill whenever he gets far enough away from the amulet that, no matter what I try, won't leave my pocket. Does that mean he's safe? I really fucking hope so.

Of course, I'm not that much of an idiot. I lock myself into my bedroom with Daisy, Stewie, and a litter box, just in case. Then, in the safety of my bedroom, I try to figure out what makes the golden coin work.

I see firsthand that it always returns to my pocket. I take it out, put it on my dresser, take off my coat, and it reappears in the pocket of my jeans. I trade my jeans for my sweats, and it pops up in that pocket. I shimmy down to my underwear, willing to sleep in my panties and nothing else to prove a point to myself, then slip my hand under my pillow only to discover that that's where the amulet is now.

After that, I give up. Yanking my sweats back on, feeling the weight of the coin as it reappears in that pocket, I try to go to sleep. I get maybe five hours down, six if I'm lucky, before I stare at my ceiling, trying to figure out what I'm going to do next.

My alarm clock does off at eight o'clock on the dot every morning. I still don't have a clue when the ringing begins. Jabbing the screen angrily, I toss the phone and climb out of my bed. A shower, I think. The warm water spraying on my back, the solitude of the stall... that'll help me figure it out.

Two steps into the bathroom and I flick the light switch on. I'm just about to slip my t-shirt on over my head when a flash of an unusual color catches my attention out of the corner of my eye. It looks like the neon green grass you usually find in a child's Easter basket. I grab it, with the intent of seeing what it is, then wince when I realize it's stuck to my head and that small little tug really hurt.

It hits me a second later. With my stomach dropping down to my bare feet, I jerk my head up and meet the rectangular mirror that hangs over my vanity.

I scream. I don't even care that it's an unholy scream, a shriek of bloody terror.

A *crash*, then a *bang*, followed by someone thundering down the hall before bursting into my bedroom.

"Maddie— Jesus, Mary, and Joseph, what happened to your hair?"

So he sees it, too. He sees that my normally honey blonde hair is a shocking, vibrant neon fucking green. I don't even know how something like that could happen? I tried to put pale purple streaks in my hair when I was a kid and it took three hours in the salon's chair just to bleach my hair light enough for the color to take.

My whole damn head is this same crazy shade. And he's the mischievous mythical creature with the magic and a hard-on for me because I "stole" his coin.

"What did you do to it?" I demand.

"Me?" Killian actually has the nerve to look surprised that I'm accusing him. "Why would you think *I* had something to do with it?"

"I told you: I didn't take your coin. You're staying in my home, isn't that enough? You didn't have to do this."

"I didn't!"

"Yeah? Prove it!"

"You're insane, woman. I told you last night, I'm a leprechaun. The only magic I have is dedicated to your wishes and, unless you wished to look like some Irish version of a troll doll, you've only got my word that I couldn't have done this. Besides, *why* would I do that? Me not feelin' as sick as a dog is only for as long as I stay in your good graces. Believe me, Maddie, angerin' you this way is the last thing I want to do."

He's got a point. Once again, I hate to admit it, but he's got a point.

He's also staring at my hair. His expression is a mix of pity, wonder, and humor. I have half a mind to grab the thing nearest to me—my toothpaste—I have half a mind to grab my toothpaste and chuck it at him. He's so obviously trying not to laugh at me. The fact that he struggles to keep a straight face but ultimately manages to is the only reason he doesn't get slapped in the face with a tube of Crest.

"Maybe it's some weird reaction to the amulet," he offers, his lips twitching just enough to have me reconsidering. "Instead of turning your skin green like cheap gold does, maybe it got to your hair?"

That's not funny. I decide to grab the toothpaste

anyway, throwing it at his wide chest instead of his face.

"Get out!" I shout.

Smart man. Without another quip, Killian turns tail and disappears.

IT'S QUIET. *TOO* QUIET.

I haven't seen either of my girls since last night. I know they were in my room with me when I locked the door. Considering how wary they are of Killian—because they have taste, obviously—it's a good bet they're still there.

But where is my unwanted guest?

He's been missing ever since I freaked out over my new hair color. He really is a smart man. I'm still so incredibly livid over the neon green, even if I had to admit that he's right. There's no way he could have done it; not on purpose, at least. I'm convinced this has goddamn leprechaun magic all over it, but he'd have to be a fucking moron to think it was a good idea to turn my hair green. I like to think I'm not vain, but it's *green*.

After I scrubbed my hair seven times, hoping the color might begin to wash out, I had to accept that it's not going anywhere anytime soon. Just like Killian, it seems. And, yeah, I'm not about to leave my apartment looking like this, either. What would my neighbors think?

Forget my neighbors for a second. How could I ever explain this to Sheila? She knows me too well. Not only would she never buy that I decided to dye my hair for yesterday's holiday, but it hit me during my last rinse that it's not like I can actually go down to our new kitchen and leave Killian behind unless I want him to suffer. And I might be really pissed off at him right now, but that doesn't mean I want him to be puking his guts up all day.

I can't bring him with me. He can't stay here without me. That only leaves me one option: I call Sheila up and tell her that the reason I was feeling tired last night was because I came down with something. Since I know she's concerned with catching the flu, I use that as an excuse. When she tells me to stay in bed, drink a lot of fluids, and get some rest, I know I've bought some time.

Now where is Killian? He's quiet, and I might not know him at all, but a quiet stranger in my house can't be a good sign.

Throwing my green hair up in a ponytail so that it's out of my face—out of sight, out of mind—I get dressed and go searching for Killian. I just about have a heart attack when I find him sitting at my dining room table, hunched over my puzzle.

"No. Don't!"

He finishes putting two pieces together as if it's the most natural thing in the world. Then, as soon as he's done, he glances up at me, his eyes flickering to my hair. He looks concerned, though he's trying to hide it.

"What's wrong, Maddie? Ah, I see your hair's still a lovely shade of green."

I ignore him. It's harder to do than last night since, I notice, his thick Irish accent is a little easier for me to understand today. Either I'm getting used to him, or he's dialed it back some. Doesn't matter.

What does matter?

I point at the puzzle. He's managed to put together a good hundred pieces in the time since I was working on it last.

"How did you do that?" I demand. "Magic?"

"I like puzzles."

Of course he does.

Why wouldn't the gorgeous man with the killer Irish accent, massive biceps, alluring green eyes, and Faerie blood *not* be a fan of the one thing that I love to do most in this world? Because if he wasn't already like a catnip made just for me, this puts it over the top.

And I can't get rid of him because he gets sick whenever he gets too far away from his amulet—and, by extension, *me*.

Ah, hell. I'm fucking doomed.

7

SEDUCTION? WHAT SEDUCTION?

Killian

Six days.

I've been in Salem for six days.

Six days, and if I don't do something about this crackling chemistry between us, I'm going to explode.

I know Maddie can sense it. While we're watching television together, while she's cooking up supper, while we settle down to work on her monster cat puzzle... there's no way she can't feel it. It's as obvious as her neon green hair, even if I have enough tact not to point that out.

It's all I can think about, too. Once she got past the idea that I wasn't going anywhere—that I really *can't*—Maddie let down her guard enough for me to get to know the woman she really is when she isn't in a rush or being bossed around by a half-blood leprechaun. The more I learn about her, the more I like. The closer we get, the more I realize that I can't leave until I have this woman at least once.

Too bad that the chances of that happening are as good as the Yankees finally showing the Red Sox up anytime this decade. Good for my Sox. All around shite for poor Killian.

This is more than my regular run of bad luck, too. There is definitely something else at play here. Pity that I can't do anything about it. Now that I'm looking at it from Maddie's point of view, I realize how terrible this has all been for her. And it's all my fault. Not the best way to convince a human I'm worth a tumble in her bed.

I mean, first, she had a stranger showing up out of the blue, demanding room and board all because she had the misfortune to pick up a lost coin. She wanted to send me away, but I went ahead and shocked her by shrinking down to my leprechaun size, abruptly introducing her to the idea that magic exists in her orderly little world, before guilt tripping her into letting me stay.

And now I'm afraid I've blown any chance I could've had with her because I was so damn insistent on getting my foot in the door so that I could get my amulet back. One thing I discovered about Maddie? Not a fan of pushy fellas.

I really wanted to blame my bad luck for it. I almost wish I could—except, apart from the whole not being able to grant wishes thing, I haven't had one unlucky thing happen to me since I started staying with Maddie.

For the first few days, I was wary of disaster striking. In my experience, if it's not a couple small things going wrong for me, it's because the magic is saving up for a doozy. I'm super careful when I'm working on Maddie's puzzle, but it never falls. When we're baking together in the kitchen—okay, when *she's* baking, and I'm keeping her company—I almost expect the stove to blow up. Nothing.

Almost a week later and I still have my left shoe.

It's all so weird, just like Maddie said. As a half-blood leprechaun, I'm used to weird—but I'm used to a certain kind of it. Having things go right for once? It's worrying me.

So then I wonder if maybe it's transferred to Maddie now that she's got my amulet. Makes sense, especially after the way her hair turned green overnight. It took two whole days before I was able to really convince her that I had nothing to do with it. Thank Éire that it's finally starting to fade a little; instead of neon green, it's a softer sort of olive color.

But nothing's gone wrong for me. In fact, as far as I'm concerned, this is the best luck I've ever had. That's not saying much for regular folks, but for a half-blood leprechaun? It's a noticeable difference—at first. Until I'm stuck inside with Maddie and I realize that being this close to her might be the worst thing that's ever happen to me. Because Maddie? She still acts like she wants me gone.

I'm beginning to think my bad luck has everything to do with how desperate I am for this woman—and how she is going to any lengths to pretend that she doesn't feel the same.

Jesus, I'm praying she feels the same. She has to, right? I mean, my luck can't be *that* awful.

I never thought I'd be the type of man who'd settle down; my ancestry almost guaranteed that I'd be a confirmed bachelor. Female leprechauns are few and far between, and me being half human meant I'd never be a good mate for any of them. Killian Finnegan is fine for a good time, but nothing serious. I've heard it all my life—even from humans, and if that ain't a kick in the ass, I don't know what is. To be fair, I've never actually even met a female leprechaun myself before, but after having a whirl with a couple of tooth fairies, a witch, and a siren I met on a trip to Katama Beach, I know what to expect from those touched by magic like me.

Humans were always a fling, since I couldn't actually come out and tell them the truth about who and what I am; Maddie's the only exception since she found my amulet and I had to fill her in. I figured a magical woman would be the way to go.

I even tried to actually have a relationship with someone like me once. Leah. She was a tooth fairy. It... didn't go well. She had a weird teeth thing, liked to bite sometimes when she was sucking my cock. And that was on the rare occasion she actually had a night off and could spend it with me. She spent so much time on the job, I barely saw her, and when my bad luck had me sitting on her wee fairy wand and snapping it in half with my ass, she said it would be better if we saw other people.

After that, I would often pick up some of the beauties who came by Finnegan's, and sometimes take them up on their offers of a fun time, but that's all it ever was. Eventually, I started to pass them off on Jer. After a while, it wasn't worth it. I needed more. Didn't know what—

—and then I met Maddie.

There's so much about her that I enjoy. She's gorgeous, devoted to her job and her cats, and one of the most hardworking people I know. She's smart as hell, plus the way she talks like a sailor sometimes makes me feel right at home. My dad would love her. She cooks almost as good as my mom. And she's got a heart of pure fucking gold to put up with me.

And, okay, I absolutely adore the way she scrunches her nose when I manage to piss her off.

Like today. I had to do it. Maybe it's ridiculous, and maybe it's a touch childish, but I don't like it when Maddie is ignoring me. Half the time, she's not even doing it on purpose. She has her own life, one that I'm definitely distracting her from; just because I'm her unwanted guest, that's not stopping her from what she'd be doing if I wasn't here.

It doesn't take Maddie long to realize there's a reason I work the bar at Finnegan's and not the kitchen. I'm real shite when it comes to instructions so my food is often edible at best. So while she spends most of her afternoons in the kitchen, prepping meals for us or for her job, I'm not allowed to help. She tells me I can find something else to entertain me, giving me free rein when it comes to her television and her bookshelves, but I don't feel right when she's not around.

Instead of meandering like a bum around her house, I use the amulet's curse as an excuse to sit at her kitchen table and keep her company. Every now and then she seems to remember me, just like when she asks me to hand her the small prep bowl containing her perfectly pre-measured out salt.

There's three bowls she left on the far counter: sugar, salt, and pepper. Even I can tell the two crystals apart. Feeling a little mischievous, I grab the sugar.

"Here you go."

"Thanks— hang on." Just before she goes to add it

to her mixture, she pauses. I'm glad. I didn't actually want to *ruin* her recipe. "This isn't the salt, Killian. It's the sugar."

"Was it really? I didn't realize."

I go for absolutely innocent. Usually, with my accent this mellowed, I can come off as charming no matter if I'm telling the tallest of tales. Not with Maddie. Never with Maddie. It's like she expects every word out of my mouth to be a lie. And that might've been, so maybe she has a right to glare up at me like that, but when her nose wrinkles in just the way I like, I can't help it.

I wait for Maddie to set the bowl gingerly down, grab the one container holding the salt, then plop the contents into her mixer. The second her back is turned, purposely ignoring me, I pounce. I grab her by the shoulders, spin her around, and angle my head until my lips are centimeters away from hers.

I hesitate for a heartbeat, breathing in her breath, her scent, waiting for her to move her head or even shove me away. When she doesn't, I close the tiny gap that remains between us, kissing her with all of the simmering attraction I've been trying to deny these last few days.

The second I pull back from her and see the anger warring with heat written on her face, I wonder if I made a terrible mistake. I'm so pent up that I'm ready to explode, but if I pushed Maddie too far, too fast? If I fucked this up before I really had a chance to make a go of it? I'll know it's all my fault.

I won't even get to blame my bad luck. That was all me and how bad I want this woman. Seduction? What seduction? Maddie looked at me like she wanted to kill me and what did I do? I kissed her.

So she kissed me back. Was it because I caught her off guard? Maybe. Don't care.

I'd do it again in a heartbeat. Éire willing, I'll get to do it a hundred times more.

Her chest is heaving and I stare, watching the rise and fall of her tits as she pants. I still don't know if she's turned on or about to let me have it. I suspect Maddie isn't quite sure, either. But she's not hitting me or shoving me away so I think I might have a real chance here.

It's a gamble. With as bad as my luck is, I should've learned long ago not to go betting when I can't afford to lose. And I can't afford to lose Maddie, not when I'm this fucking close to getting another taste.

I want more.

I want it *all*.

Grabbing her ass with my hands, I hoist her up, urging her to wrap her legs around my waist. I'm holding her in my palms, careful not to squeeze her cheeks; as tempting as that is, as hot and horny as I am, I don't want Maddie to ever think she doesn't have a choice. So when she settles her weight in my hands, locking her ankles behind my back, I don't do anything more than angle my hips, letting the bulge in my jeans hit her right between her legs.

Maddie lets out a throaty moan that nearly has me creaming myself. Throwing her head back, her long wavy hair falling in waves down her back, she loses herself in the sensation as she grinds herself on my length. It feels so fucking good, I can't stop myself from groaning along with her.

You know, I kind of think she forgot that I was here as she basically tried to ride me like I was a horse. The groan brings her down to earth. Her blue eyes seem dazed as she focuses on me. Her lips are pouting, plus they're a little puffy from the force of our earlier kiss.

She looks so damn tempting. God, I want to kiss her again.

"I can't stand you," she spits out before she grabs my face roughly and pulls me in toward her. Her lips slam into mine, oue teeth clacking, tongues tangling as she kisses me in that single-minded certainty that's all Maddie.

8

ALL FOR HER

Killian

SHE DOESN'T HATE ME.

I'm absolutely sure of it. I might piss her off, and I might enjoy doing it on purpose, but I'm not a masochist. If I didn't think that Maddie was feeling the same pull toward me that I felt toward her, I never would've laid a hand on her.

And, right now, my hands are on her ass and, good lord, I'm in heaven. As she kisses me madly, desperately, twining her tongue with mine, I knead my fingers against her ass cheeks and pull her toward me. I angle my hips again, pressing her against my aching cock, and kiss her as if my life depends on it.

It might. If not my life, then definitely my balls. If I

don't get inside this woman and *soon*, they're likely to fall right off. I'm not even fucking kidding.

My blood is pumping, rushing through my veins, heading straight to my cock. I'm as hard as the blessed Blarney Stone, I swear it, and as long as she's clutching me, her nails biting into my back, I'm going to do everything I can to convince her to give it a goddamn kiss.

But this is Maddie—my Maddie, even if she doesn't know I'm claiming her just yet—and I know exactly how to get her going. Only, this time, I'm not looking for an argument or a way to rile her up because it turns me on. I want to rev her up, make her lose herself in her fury, make her lose herself in *me*. I'm a desperate man. My bad luck will mess this up for me eventually. For as long as I have her in my arms, I'm going to make the best of it.

Taking her bottom lip between my teeth, I give her a quick nip. Not to hurt her, because I'd never do that to her, but just enough to keep her on her toes.

When she gasps in surprise, I murmur, "Keep telling yourself that, sweetheart," before darting my tongue out and giving the small pain a quick, soothing lick.

Her chest heaving, tits rising and falling with her panted breaths, Maddie sucks her bottom lip into her mouth, lathing the exact point where my tongue just was. Lust has turned her blue eyes a darker shade as her pupils dilate. A blush rises high on her pale cheeks. She's staring at me now.

She's got to see the need written in every line of my face. Her eyes flicker down to the bulge in my jeans. The denim is containing my erection, but there's no hiding the fact that I'm ready and raring to go. She knows it, too, otherwise she wouldn't keep riding against me like that.

There's a moment, a fucking awful heartbeat, when I think she's going to tell me to let her go or maybe put her down.

Instead, she shakes her head. "We shouldn't do this. We really shouldn't do this. It would be a mistake. You know that, right?"

"Aye."

"We shouldn't do this," she says again, before darting her tongue out, licking her bottom lip enticingly.

If she's waiting for me to agree again, she'll be waiting forever.

I raise my eyebrows. "But we're gonna, aren't we?"

I hold my breath. Maddie looks me right in the eyes and, just when I'm afraid I'm about to pass out from lack of oxygen, she nods.

Hell fucking yes!

I'm not about to give her the chance to change her mind. I steal her lips again, kissing her so that she stays focused on me and now what's about to happen. I know Maddie. She tends to overthink things, even when they're as simple as this. Using my right hand to guide me, I stumble out of the kitchen, still supporting Maddie with my left hand. I duck her head, urging her to kiss my neck while I maneuver the two of us up the stairs and into her bedroom.

Except for the quick glance I got the day she screamed because her hair was green, I haven't seen Maddie's room. It's bigger than the guest room, and tastefully furnished, with a big floor lamp, two dressers, a night stand, and a cozy queen-size bed.

I zero right in on it, gently laying Maddie down on the edge of the mattress. The second she's free, she reaches for her jeans. The sound of her zipper as she tugs it down is like music to my ears.

I watch as she shimmies out of them, tossing her pants to the side, before slipping her fingers beneath the band of her pretty pink panties. My cock is aching so badly, I hurry to let it out. By the time Maddie is reaching up to remove her shirt, I've got my jeans down around my ankles, my boxers right on top. I kick off my shoes, shake loose my clothes, then add my t-shirt to the pile.

Once I'm bare-assed naked, my cock pointing straight up, I realize my mistake. Letting lust cloud my head is all well and good until I'm about to climb on top of a willing woman. Still, I've got to think with the brain in my head, not just the one in my dick. Holding up a finger so that Maddie knows I'll be right back, I dash down the hall to my room and grab my duffel bag from the floor.

When it became clear that I wasn't leaving anytime soon, I borrowed the dresser in Maddie's guest room and unpacked the few changes of clothes I brought with me. Since it was always really damn obvious that the box I packed was nothing but wishful thinking, I left it in the duffel. I might have never expected her to sleep with me in a thousand years after the bad start we had, but I guess I'm nothing if not hopeful.

I run back to Maddie to discover that she's fully naked, and also sitting cross-legged on the bed as if she's suddenly having second thoughts. If I don't act quick, she could easily grab her comforter and cover up the magnificent view she's letting me have.

Then her eyebrows fly high when she catches sight of the box in my hand and I wonder if I've already fucked this up beyond repair.

"Condoms? Why do you have those?"

Her suspicious, demanding nature shouldn't be such an aphrodisiac. Ripping the box open, I pull out a strip and tear one off the end. I toss the rest on her nightstand since I have every intention of running through as many as I can before she stops me.

Keep it breezy, Kill. Keep it light.

My fingers fumble as I fiddle with the condom, but I offer her a cheeky grin so that she doesn't think I'm as desperate as I am. "I'm a leprechaun, sweetheart, but I was a boy scout, too. Always be prepared."

Maddie's nose wrinkles and, fuck it, I'm prepared to beg when she lets out a sigh. "Okay. I know that's a line, but right now? I don't give a shit. Slip that sucker on and get over here before I realize this is fucking nuts and change my mind."

"Your wish is my command, sweetheart."

I don't expect the pillow she tosses at my face, but as the silky pillowcase slams into my cheek right as I'm finally tearing open the foil packet, I have to admit I deserved that. The pillow falls to the floor and I kick it absently aside. I grab my cock, rolling the condom over my length. I'm already leaking pre-cum, I'm so ready to explode. Six days of pent-up sexual need is torture. I'm used to getting laid the same night I meet an attractive woman. Coming too quickly, finishing my time with her before it's really begun, is a serious concern.

But I have to make this good for her. I have to make this last. I give my cock a leisurely stroke, enjoying the feel of the rubber against my overheated skin, then squeeze the base of my shaft in order to get control of my need.

Then, when I'm feeling like a brush of her hand won't be enough to set me off like a rocket, I give her an order. "Spread your legs, Maddie."

Her eyes dip to the dark blonde curls covering her pussy. "Are you going to—"

"Do you want me to?" I lick my lips because the ideas of tasting her is so fucking hot, I can't stop myself. But I have to make sure she wants it. This is me proving myself. "Because, just bein' honest, I'm dyin' to."

She scoots back eagerly, using the remaining pillows on her bed to prop her back up against the headboard. With an excited squeal, she lets her legs fall open, then closes her eyes.

I dive right in. Using my hands to spread her thighs, I reveal her pussy for the first time. It's as pretty and pink as her panties were, glistening enticingly as I get my first idea of just how wet she is. Any doubt I might've harbored about her doing this out of pity or boredom is gone in an instant.

My Maddie is as horny for me as I am for her. Look at all those juices. With one long lick up her slit, I take as much in as I can. She tastes fucking *amazing*. I increase the force of my lick, dipping the tip of my tongue into her entrance, gathering more of her juices before searching for her clit.

And then I attack it.

Sucking the pearl into my mouth, swirling my tongue around it before giving her another long, loving lick, I keep Maddie on the edge for as long as I dare. From above me, I hear her moaning my name in between threatening all the things she's going to do to my cock if I don't get on with it and give her some release.

So I do.

She tries to shove my head away from her when she gets close, but I'm not done yet. I give her one final lick. Maddie gasps and, suddenly, my head is locked in the vice of her thighs. She rides out her orgasm on my face, my nose buried in her curls, my mouth lavishing the stiff bud of her clit. I start to feel a little light-headed as her legs shake, but if this is how I'm going to die?

Good heaven, what a way to go.

I nuzzle her pussy when the orgasm passes. This time, when she pushes me away because she's too sensitize, I let her. Her juices cover my face. I lick my lips, gathering the last of it, then wipe my mouth, my nose, and my cheeks to get the rest. My hand is slick. After I run my pointer finger up her slit, checking to see that she's ready for me, I cover the rubber with my hand. I'm a big man and Maddie, for all her personality, is kind of tiny. A little extra lube won't hurt.

She's still on her back, big blue eyes staring up at me in something close to wonder. I let slip my smirk. If that made her feel good, she hasn't seen anything yet.

Grabbing my cock by the base again, I put a little pressure on it before swing my leg over her hip, covering her with my entire body. I line my cock up at her entrance, then lean on my elbow as I begin to push inside of her.

I meet enough resistance to tell me that it's been a while for Maddy, too. For some irrational reason, that makes me happy. I push a little more, taking care to watch her face as she adjusts to my width. She's breathing softly, but she's smiling, and when she nods again, I know she's ready. She's already got half of my cock inside of her. With a smirk, I slam all the way home.

Oh, Éire, she's tight and she's wet and if I thought I found heaven in her kisses, I've discovered paradise in her pussy. I don't ever want to leave and, as I pull back, I thrust right back in.

We find a frantic, messy rhythm almost immediately. Without me even urging her to, Maddie wraps her legs around me again, digging her heels in my ass as she clutches my shoulders. I can feel the bite of her fingernails in my shoulder blades as I continue to pound into her. She begs for more and I give her everything I have.

In that moment, as I bring her to her peak again before following closely behind her, I know that there's something about Maddie Scott. She's a perfect fit for me, whether she knows it or not. In the bedroom. Out of it. I'll give her everything I have—

Now, if only she'll take it.

9

INEVITABLE

Maddie

I DON'T REGRET IT.

It's the first thing that hits me when I wake up the next morning, my legs intertwined with Killian's, my head resting against his bicep. No lie, he smells like a mix of sweat, Irish Spring soap, and something utterly manly—something utterly *him*. I'm sure I smell like it, too.

After our first frantic, primal coupling, I tried to escape him by taking a shower. I definitely needed one. Killian didn't let me.

Oh, he didn't stop me. I could have gotten away from him at any time. Only thing is, I didn't *want* to. So I climbed back into my bed and, when Killian asked me if I wouldn't mind doing that with him again, I was all for it.

Three times. I slept with Killian three times before he snuggled up next to me and finally let me, well, actually *sleep*. One arm tucked under my head, the other wrapped around my waist, Killian held me close after he got up and disposed of the last condom. Whatever he thought of what happened between us—a one-night stand, hate sex, or momentary insanity—the way he cuddled after we were both finished? I can't regret it.

And I don't.

Maybe he was right. He told me it was inevitable after the first time I came and he finished. Inevitable because even I wasn't so blind to the sparks between us. Inevitable because it had been years since I let myself go like that. Inevitable because Killian's Irish accent and stunning smile had me getting wet the first time we ever met, before I decided he was a jerk. Jury's still out on that at times, but after all those nights we sat together, working on puzzles and learning about each other, it really was inevitable, wasn't it?

He didn't need any kind of Faerie magic to lure me in. His crooked smile and that come hither look in his eyes did more to entice me to follow him to bed than any magic spell ever could. I can admit now that I've been a goner since that first second I caught sight of him standing behind Finnegan's counter. He stopped me in my tracks then just as easily as he did when he kissed me last night.

It was inevitable, and it was magical, and I'm going to have to be very careful that it doesn't happen again.

It can't. Though I don't regret it, falling into bed with Killian was a mistake because all I'm thinking about right now is doing it again. His body could become addictive, the passion and the drive and, my God, his fucking stamina—but that's not even the worst of it. The cuddling. The damn cuddling. The way he held me afterward, snuggling close, keeping me in his arms as if he couldn't bear to let me go? I liked it. A lot. A girl could get used to that.

Giving into our noticeable sexual tension is one thing. It's... it's a biological urge, right? Having sex with a gorgeous man like Killian for the pleasure and the release is one thing. But the cuddling... the way he murmured such sweet things as he pounded into me... how he whispered *Maddie* every time he reached his orgasm.

Okay. So maybe I'm no expert at relationships. Once I hit thirty last year, I pretty much gave in to the idea that I'd be settling down with my cats. I was all for it. I love my girls. But Killian?

It would be too, too easy to fall for him, too.

Ugh. I always get so mopey and introspective after sex. It's one reason I never took Sheila's advice to go out for the night, find a stranger, and get boned. As much as I tried to, I just can't separate my pussy from my heart. It's like, I let a man into one, it's not too long before I stop wondering if I've given him a way into the other.

Suddenly, I don't think I can stand being so close to him. I could handle the angry sex. What I can't handle? Having him continue to hold me close as if what happened between us actually *means* something to him.

I'm just about to disentangle myself from his embrace when I hear Killian make a soft hushing noise. He's... he's awake. He's awake and, unless I'm imagining it, his arms have tightened a little in the last few seconds.

Now, I'm not usually a chickenshit. That's not who I am, and I think he knows that by now. But when I realize he's awake, I totally fake falling back asleep. Though my heart is racing—because he's awake and, damn it, he's still cuddling me as if he doesn't have any regrets, either—I try to slow my breathing down to appear as if I'm sleeping again. I relax my eyes so that it doesn't seem like they're squinted shut.

I stay like that for a couple of minutes. The time goes slow as I wait to see how Killian will react. Bastard actually snuggles closer, nuzzling his chin in my messy, tangled hair, before nosing me against my cheek, my ear, then pressing his lips sweetly to the hollow of my throat. And he stays like that, breathing softly against my skin, unaware of the shivers I'm trying to to hide. I almost think he's fallen back to sleep, too, when I hear a high-pitched *meow,* followed by a softer, more throaty *mrow*.

The girls. They'll be needing their breakfast.

I hear Killian groan. Of course. He barely tolerates my girls at the best of times. Before I can pull away from him, getting up to take care of Daisy and Stew while saving them from Killian's evil eye and nasty comments, he slips his arm out from under me and stealthily slips out of the bed.

I hear his bare feet slapping against the wooden floor of my bedroom. Another groan, another cry from one of the cats, then a muttered, "Give me a sec, sweetheart. I'd rather not let my dick hang out like one of your toys, alright? Just need my boxers."

A rustle of clothing, the pitter patter of little paws. I know exactly what they're doing. When Daisy and Stewie are desperate for their morning and evening meals, they swarm me, circling my ankles while crying until I put their food down.

Problem is, I don't know what the hell *Killian* is doing. And I'm dying to figure it out.

The bed bounces like a small weight has been dropped on it. It's harder to keep my eyes closed but something tells me to. The comforter shifts as one of the girls starts padding toward me.

I sense someone else coming close. A soft *yowl* and

a quick breeze is a pretty good clue that Killian came over and swooped the wayward kitty up off of the bed.

"Come on, sweetheart. Let's let Mama sleep, yeah?" He lets out a soft chuckle, obviously careful not to wake me, then tells my cat, "I wore her out, so it's only fair if I let her get some rest. But I'm bettin' you're hungry, Daisy. Don't worry. I'll make sure you're fed."

I can't help it. Even though I'm risking Killian calling me out for faking, I peek open my eye.

He's standing on his side of the bed, wearing his boxers and that's it. Normally, getting an eyeful of his nearly naked body would mean that I was staring at his beautiful, masculine form. Not today—and not only because his chest is blocked by the tortoiseshell cat he's holding close to his chest.

Holy. Shit.

Killian has Daisy in his arms, tickling her chin just the way she likes before rubbing her ear, then scratching her scruff. The old girl is putty in his hands. Even from across the room, I can hear the motor-like sound of her content purring.

I don't need to get a peek at her tail to know that the cat he's holding is Daisy. What amazes me, though? *He* knows that it's Daisy.

And she *likes* him.

Keeping Daisy tucked under his arm, Killian bends slightly, using his free hand to give Stewie a sweet pat on her head. She's the kitty with the high-pitched *meow*; Kill laughs when she lets out another screech. It really does sound like a demand.

"Yes, Ms. Stew. You'll be getting some breakfast, too, my girl. Come on. Let's go get your food before we wake Maddie up. But do me a favor, yeah? When Mama gets up, let's keep this between the three of us. You might get another breakfast out of it, and Lord knows she'll never believe it anyway. Remember our pact. No one eats me when I'm small, and I sneak you treats whenever I can. Alright..."

His voice fades the further he goes from the room. And, okay, I know Killian is a talker. The man never shuts the hell up. To hear him talking to my cats? I'm not all that surprised. He'd talk to the walls if he thought they were listening. I guess it's what makes him such a great bartender.

But he's still talking to Daisy and Stewie as he heads downstairs. It's not a show for me—like my cynical nature expected for a moment—otherwise he would've stopped before he was out of earshot. He was talking to my girls because, as much as he tried to hide it from me these last few days, I think he actually cares for them. Not surprising. They're awesome cats—even if Daisy did try to eat Killian once. Still, the warm, contented feeling that rushes through me as I think of how amazing he looked with Daisy in his arms, leaving the cozy bed in order to feed my girls so that I wasn't disturbed?

Oh, man. I'm in *trouble*.

Flopping onto my back, I lay my head against my rumpled pillow and stare at the ceiling. No reason to pretend to be sleeping now. With the thoughts running through my head, I don't think I could've faked it convincingly any way.

Did I think that it would be easy to let him into my heart?

Motherfucker. I'm beginning to suspect he already *has* it.

Killian

I go downstairs and feed Maddie's cats, taking care to make sure to give Daisy more wet food than Stewie since she's older and the soft food is easier to digest. It makes me laugh now to think that she's the fierce beastie that came at me when I was shrunk down to my leprechaun size. Now that I know her, I figure it was more of a shock to her than it was to me. She's a sweet old girl. She never would've eaten me, not the way Maddie spoils her.

Maddie. Ah. Thank Éire that she's still sleeping. I can just imagine her accusing me of poisoning her cats or some shite. Just because she let me fuck her, it doesn't mean that her opinion of me is going to change overnight. That's okay. I'm up for the challenge.

Besides, it's not as if I'm going anywhere anytime

soon. Heading down to the kitchen while Maddie stays in the bedroom is about as far as I can go from her without feeling any ill effects from the magic.

From the *magic*. Having her out of my sight affects me in a totally different way. The human male that I am finds it... difficult to be too far from the woman.

I might've been able to ignore how she made me feel if we hadn't given into our mutual urge to sleep together last night—even if we didn't really do all that much sleeping. Now? Now that I know what it's like to get inside of Maddie? I'm extremely eager to do it again. And again.

After putting a fresh bowl of water down for the cat, I give each one a pat, then head back upstairs. If I'm lucky, Maddie's still knocked out and I can slip into bed without her ever knowing that I left. Even if I only get to hold her in my arms, I'll be happy.

The bed is empty when I let myself into her room. Damn it. I can hear the water from her shower running; the door is closed so I take the hint that morning shower sex isn't in my future. It's a shame. With the tent forming in my boxers, I'm more than ready for some.

I'm not going to push, though. I know I got lucky last night—and I mean that in more than one way. Maddie could've lashed out at me when I kissed her like that. I'm so glad she didn't, and I'm just hoping last night was as good for her as it was for me so that she'll be open to the idea of a repeat.

Since I have nothing better to do—and a quick check of my pits tells me I'm smelling a little ripe—I gather up my clothes from Maddie's floor and return to the guest room. I take a quick shower, throwing on my favorite, weathered Red Sox t-shirt—the one celebrating the ten-year anniversary of the team winning the 2004 World Series—over a pair of comfy jeans, and head downstairs to wait for her.

WHEN MADDIE COMES DOWN ABOUT AN HOUR LATER, I put down the book I'm reading and wait to see what she's going to say to me.

After clearing her throat, she says, "Since we finally finished the cat puzzle last night, I thought we could start another one. It's not a ten thousand piece puzzle like the other one, and I still need to put the puzzle glue down and it takes time to set, but I have an easy five hundred piece puzzle we can do on the kitchen table, if you want."

It's not a declaration of love or even an invitation to drop my boxers and whip out my cock. I get the vibe that she's pointedly choosing not to talk about last night. At least she's not ignoring me. Working on a puzzle together? Okay. I'll take it.

"No cookin' today?" I ask cheerfully, rising up from the couch in order to join her in the kitchen.

She shakes her head. "I hate lying to Sheila, but she still thinks I'm sick. She only let me have a couple of orders because I begged her and, I'm betting, deep down she realizes that I'm perfectly healthy. I finished it all yesterday morning. I'll have to call her later for some work."

"You're going to have to go back eventually, though, right?"

As she grabs the box of puzzle pieces from the top of her refrigerator, she tosses a peeved look at me from over her shoulder. "What will I do with you then? You want to spend the days puking your guts up in my bathroom while I'm at work?"

"Hey, I'm a talented mixologist. Maybe you can hire me to work for your catering service and I can come along with you."

Maddie mumbles something under her breath, almost like *and it's not like Sheila didn't bring on an employee without me*, before plopping the box on the edge of her table. "I don't know. We'll see. For now, I guess we're both stuck here together."

She sounds so miserable. Maybe I really am a masochist because the idea of being forced to spend all of my time with Maddie is one of the only good things to come out of losing my damn amulet.

After covering the table with a large swath of wax

paper, she asks me if I'm ready to get started with the puzzle. It's a clear signal that she wants to drop the conversation. I go along with it, letting her think she's been granted a reprieve, even if I have every intention of returning to the conversation later.

For now, we work on the puzzle. It's only five hundred pieces, but the puzzle is a picture of a haunted forest and all of the blasted trees look the same. It takes all of our concentration and, pretty soon, a hush has fallen over the kitchen.

Which is why, a couple of hours later when we're halfway done with the puzzle, the sudden knocking, followed by the loud shrieking nearly has me jumping out of my skin. Maddie actually gives a jolt, her hand shaking so bad that she messes up the corner next to her.

"Madison Elaine Scott! Open this door up right now or I'll knock it down!"

10

CUPID'S BLESSING

Maddie

"Sheila," I realize. "It's Sheila. Shit."

I should've been expecting this. If I'm being honest, I kind of thought she would've hunted me down long before this. It's why I fibbed and said I thought I had the flu. Sheila's sweet, but she's also terrified of coming down with something that'll knock her on her ass. After telling me that I needed to rest and relax and take care of myself to get better, she promised to bring me soup if I asked her to then told me she'd see me again when I was feeling better.

I guess a week was long enough for her to get over her fears of me being contagious. And I know Sheila. If I don't open that door and let her in, she really will break the damn thing down.

"Stay here," I tell Killian. "I'll be right back."

I don't even have to hear the squeak of his chair as he shoves it away from the table to know that he's right on my ass as I head to the front door. Figuring it's not worth the argument—I know I would win, but Sheila might make good on her threat before it's over—I lead Killian over to the front door and swing it open.

Sheilas gasps when she sees me.

"Your hair!"

Even though it's started to fade, my hair is still green. No getting around that. I guess I kind of forgot about it, though. I stopped pulling it back in ponytails because it was just me and Killian and, for some reason, he seems to like it. Probably because it *is* green.

Killian sneaks up right behind me. I can sense him at my back about two seconds before he lets out a cheery laugh. "Ah, don't tell me you aren't a fan of the color green, lass."

Sheila has to do a double-take. Unlike me, she's not short, so she doesn't have to tilt her head back to get a good look at Killian. To be honest, I'm no so sure she even notices how gorgeous he is, considering how she's head over heels in love with Cole. But the accent? From the way her face screws up, as if she's not sure to laugh or what, she definitely picked up on that.

Then she says, in that blunt Sheila fashion, "Shit, he sounds like he stepped right out of Darby O'Gill and the Little People."

"Most people reference Boondocks Saints," Killian says solemnly.

"Yeah? Well I'm not most people." Jerking her thumb at Killian, Sheila asks, "Who's he?"

I didn't really think I'd get away without having to make introductions. "Killian. He's—" Oh, jeez, how to explain? "He's a friend of mine. He, uh, came to take care of me while I had the flu."

Sheila raises her eyebrows. "Really? And this is the first time I'm hearing of this *friend*?"

"He's a new friend," I say firmly. Then, before she can say anything else, I turn to Killian. "This is Sheila. She runs the catering service with me. And that guy hovering behind her? That's her boyfriend."

Cole smiles apologetically when I turn back to face them. "I'm sorry, Madison. I tried to convince her not to—"

"A week!" explodes Sheila. "I let you hide in here for a week! If it was the flu, you'd either be dead or back at work by now. How was I supposed to know you had a... a friend in here? You could've told me over the phone."

"You're right. I'm sorry, Sheil. I wasn't thinking straight." That much, at least, is true. All I wanted to do was make sure that no one else knew about the mess I was in. "I blame it on the flu."

"Yeah, well, I'm glad you're feeling better, sweetie.

You've obviously got your color back, even if I might've stopped at turning my hair green."

I feel Killian's hand land on the top of my head, his fingers combing through the length of my waves. His chuckle makes his hand shake before he settles his palm against my shoulder. It's a strangely possessive gesture, and there's a hint of a challenge in his tone when he says, "I'm thinkin' green is a lovely color. And Maddie can definitely pull it off."

Cole is looking at him curiously. Biting down on his bottom lip, he hesitates for a second before blurting out, "I'm sorry. Do I know you?"

Killian

I was wondering if the cupid was going to say something, or if the two of us were going to stand there while the ladies fought with each other. When he asks if he knows me, I figure it has more to do with settling down his woman than because he's curious.

He's right, though. I remember seeing him before. The only difference? Last time he was at Finn's with Henry, his eyes were still pink. Now? They're a deep brown.

"You used to work with Henry, ain't that right? He's a pal o' mine." Letting go of Maddie for a second, I tap near my temple, motioning toward my eye, before touching her again. "I can tell it's used to on account of the ol' peepers."

Sheila looks from me to her man and back. Her eyes flash to the point where my hand is resting on Maddie's shoulder and, most shockingly, she's *letting me do it*. "Cole? You know this guy?"

The former cupid nods. "Yeah. He's a friend of a friend."

"Oh." It's like the wind goes out of Sheila's sails. Thank Éire for Cole 'cause that's all it takes. She drops the subject like it's a hot potato. "In that case, I guess it's fine."

Maddie blinks in surprise at how easy that was. "It's fine? Aren't you going to ask me why I've got a strange man in my house? Cole might know him, but don't you want to know how I do?"

Sheila turns to Cole. "Do I?"

"No." And then, as if it means something to the both of them, he adds, "I don't have my reader, but I'm still a pro. It's a good match. I told you it would work out."

Sheila beams over at us. "You heard the man. He's the expert."

"Expert at *what*?"

"You'll see." Grabbing Cole by the sleeve of his windbreaker, Sheila winks and offers Maddie a wave before she starts to back away from the porch. "Take all the time you need. Me and Cole got this. Have fun with Killian. It's about damn time."

Maddie turns bright red. I finally figure out what the cupid meant about us being a good match and I puff my chest out. I've got a cupid's blessing. I knew whatever was between us had to be real.

Preening behind her, I tip an imaginary cap in Sheila's direction. "Nice to meet you. As my people say, 'May the road rise to meet you, and the sun always be at your back.' Oh, and next time? Call ahead. We might be too busy to answer the door."

———

To my surprise, Maddie doesn't mention any of her friends' strange visit; at least, not right away. Instead, she looks up at me. Pointing a finger at my chest while wearing an accusing expression, she said, "You were putting them on, weren't you? You're Irish, but even when you're all hot and bothered, you're not *that* Irish."

I'm surprised she picked up on how thick my Irish brogue gets when she turns me on. Plus, I'm amazed she can tell the acts apart. I don't admit that, though. "Well, she's the one who mentioned the little people."

I don't know what it is I said, but Maddie laughs. A sweet laugh, high and clear, and hell if it doesn't affect me.

She's oblivious. "Can you imagine her reaction if

she found out you really were a leprechaun? Sheila would lose her shit! Not that I'll tell her—I know the only reason I found out was because of the amulet and everything, but still. I don't know if Sheila would ever believe that magic's real."

Considering her man used to be a cupid and I'm damn sure she's aware of it, I almost want to correct Maddie on that. But then she settles down a little before she goes on to say, "You know that she thinks we're sleeping together now, don't you?," and my brain goes empty.

All I can do is remember last night when I was cock deep inside of this woman. With a daring note to my voice, I say, "We did."

"Yeah. We, uh, we definitely did."

I expected her to look away when I threw that back at her, maybe to even deny it. She'd spent all morning pretending it didn't happen, after all.

But she doesn't do any of that. Instead, Maddie smiles, and the sudden emotion in her big, blue eyes makes me lose my breath. That's it. I can't help it. For the first time since we met, she's looking at me without that guarded, wary expression. That's affection written on her face, a pure joy mixed with lust that makes her seem to glow while making all of my blood head straight to my cock.

Good Lord, I've never seen anything more beautiful in my life.

Without even pausing to think about it, I grab her hand and start to pull her gently through the house.

She doesn't pull away. With a sort of confused chuckle, she asks, "Where are we going?"

Not to finish the puzzle, that's for damn sure.

I pause when we reach the stairs, lingering at the edge of them, looking down at her. I have to give her the chance to refuse. I want her like hell, but this will only be amazing if she wants me just as badly. I know she did yesterday. Last night, when we were riding high on anger, attraction, and the spark of chemistry that's been sizzling between us since the first moment we met at my dad's bar, she was definitely into me.

In her right mind, without my excellent seduction skills clouding her thoughts, will she still—

Maddie tugs on my hand. "Well, what are you waiting for? Come on."

I grin, then sweep her up in my arms. Before she can change her mind, I jog up the steps and take her to her room.

No.

To *our* room.

11

THE BANANA

Maddie

Sheila calls every day, checking in on Killian and me while filling me in on what's going on with our business.

She doesn't ask questions about what's going on between us and I'm so damn grateful, she has no idea. And that's because, honestly, *I* have no idea—at least, when it comes to this newfound shift in the strange relationship I have with Killian.

Two weeks ago, he was a stranger. Ten days ago, he was an unwanted guest.

Last week, he became the guy I fucked because I just couldn't take the temptation any longer.

And then there was last night. Last night was different. It was nice and it was sweet and, shit, that was the closest I've ever come to making love. It sounds corny, and maybe it's a cliche, but the way he tenderly entered me while gazing deep in my eyes and stroking my finally-blonde-again hair, I remember thinking: this is what making love is like.

It's like that morning with Daisy and Stew all over again, only this time I'm sure of it. Killian doesn't just have my heart. He has all of me, body and soul. And he has no idea because there's no way in hell I'm going to tell him.

I try to keep our relationship casual, instead; well, as casual as possible when we spend every minute just about attached to the hip. We cook together—rather, I cook, because Kill is a disaster in the kitchen—and we do puzzles, plus we talk. More than half the time he's doing the talking and I'm listening, but I'm used to that after being friends with Sheila all these years. Over the last two weeks, I've realized that I actually like Killian as much as I lust after him, and it sucks that I'm feeling all of these crazy emotions and he acts like he's just killing time until we can figure out why the amulet still isn't working.

And, okay, maybe there's more to it than that. But every time Killian gets that serious look on his face, like what he's going to say is going to actually affect me, I wimp out and change the subject. Or I grab his crotch and distract him with sex. Anything to keep this light and breezy because, damn it, I know it's not going to last.

How can it? He can't stay with me forever. I know that. I'm still amazed that he's managed to ditch his life in Boston for as long as he has. He swears that the bar is fully staffed without him there, and he's had a few conversations with his father in Ireland. He understands the Faerie magic even more than Killian does. His advice? Wait it out. The amulet's magic will win in the end.

And then I'll be alone.

So maybe I'm trying to keep this wall between us. I'm only trying to protect my own heart.

ONCE AGAIN, WE'RE WORKING ON A PUZZLE.

It's so nice to have someone who likes doing this with me. I always thought it was an individual activity until I met Killian, and now I'm trying to go through all of the boxes I've bought these last few years because I know damn well that, after he leaves, I'll probably never want to work on another one ever again.

We're back in the living room, working on my bigger table. This one is another ten thousand piece puzzle and, in the last few days, we've gotten the border done as well as a few corners. I'm currently focused on gathering all of the teal blue pieces together and I'm missing one with a noticeable cut.

Without glancing up, I call out to Killian: "Hey, do you have one of the water pieces with a sharp corner?"

He doesn't answer me.

I lift my head to discover that he's staring at me. When our eyes meet, a weird expression crosses his handsome face, almost like he's about to be sick. He swallows roughly.

"You okay, Kill? You're looking weird."

He shakes his head. "Yeah, sorry. I just realized something."

My stomach immediately goes tight. I don't know why, but I can sense that something's not right. Whatever he realized? It has something to do with me—and I don't like it. I have this sudden certainty that, whatever it is, I don't want to hear it. The way things are going right now are fine. I've gotten used to it.

I don't want them to change.

"Okay. So, do you have that piece?"

He's not even looking at the puzzle. "Listen, Maddie, I have to tell you something. I—"

Pop.

Killian cocks his head slightly. He has one of his hands resting in his lap. Slowly, he lifts it up so that I can see what he's holding.

It's a banana.

"What in the—"

It hits me in a flash. A *banana*. "My wish," I breathe out

A frantic look fills his face, his features twisted in a look of horror when suddenly, with another soft *pop*, Killian is gone. The banana drops down onto the puzzle, scattering a few of his pieces, but that's it. His seat is empty. He's really, really gone.

I jump up from my chair. "Killian? Killian! That's not funny! Where did you go?"

There's no answer, and that's when I remember. When he first came to my house and he kept on insisting that I make three wishes. What did I say? *I wish you would go away!*

I grab the banana. Pressing it against my chest, I yell out one more time, "Killian?"

I don't know where he is, but one thing is for sure: he's not here. That's okay, I realize. It's fine. Because I've only used two wishes. I still have one more left, right? The banana and my frustrated wish that he would leave me alone. That's only two.

"I wish you would come back."

And... nothing happens.

I immediately reach inside my pocket, already knowing what I'm going to find.

Yup.

The coin is finally gone, too.

Killian

One second, I'm staring at a banana in my hand, a pit in my stomach forming as I'm thrown back to the day I first met Maddie. The next? I'm winking out of existence, only to reappear a heartbeat later.

Without the banana.

Without Maddie, either.

Because, all of a sudden, I'm back in Boston. Not quite sure how it happened, but there's no denying it.

As disoriented as I am from the magic transporting me back, I recognize my bedroom in a flash. The Red Sox pennant pinned on the wall, the dark blue cotton sheets, the snow boots I kicked aside when I was hurriedly packing in between those awful bouts of dry heaves. It's just how I left it right before I started speeding toward the pull of my amulet—

My amulet.

I shove my hands in my jeans. My fingers close around the familiar shape, still warm with Maddie's body heat. Yanking it out, I stare at it almost disbelievingly. I have it again, in my pocket where it used to belong.

Without knowing why exactly, I squeeze the gold coin. Seconds later, it heats up to the point that it's almost burning my skin. I curse under my breath, just about to let the damn thing fall to my carpet when, I swear to Éire, I hear Maddie's voice whisper in my ears—

I wish I had someone who would love me like that.

I wish for a banana.

I wish you would go away.

Three wishes and the geis is met. The amulet is mine again.

I should be happy.

I'm not.

I'm fucking *stunned*.

That's it? That's what happened? All this time, I thought the magic wasn't working because I couldn't grant Maddie's wish. And I asked her, too. I asked her if she made a wish. Maybe she didn't remember, maybe it was a fleeting thought that passed through her head, but the magic picked up on it. Of course, it did. That's what Faerie magic does.

The second I admitted to myself that I was in love with Maddie? She got her wish. She found a man who would love her. That's why I was holding a banana in my hand in the next moment before vanishing from her apartment. Three wishes and I got my amulet back.

Three wishes and I'm home.

Well, that's not about to last. If I know Maddie, she'll start to convince herself that everything that passed between us was for fun, that we're too different to ever make this work. I wouldn't be surprised if she's already making arrangements to go straight to her kitchen, neatly putting the last two weeks behind her like the anal way she organizes her cutlery drawer.

Yeah, right. I'm not about to let her get away that easily. When I'm with Maddie, I'm not the half-blood leprechaun who hides his frustration with his shitty luck behind a cocky attitude and a need to get laid to prove I'm worth something. When I'm with Maddie, sex isn't just about getting off. It's about making that connection.

It's about being in love. And, damn it, I won't stop until she loves me, too.

The revelation of her first wish and what it actually means doesn't hit me until I've turned to race right back to her.

I wish I had someone who would love me like that.

Did... did the geis make it so that I imagined I was in love with her in order to grant her wish?

Holy fucking shite.

No. *No*. It's... it's not possible. I love her because she's Maddie and she's perfect for me and there's no way that the magic makes me think that all because she wished it.

I mean, *hell*. Even when I managed to lock myself out of my apartment a couple of years ago wearing nothing but a confused grin and my birthday suit, my luck wasn't *this* bad.

Sometimes it saved it all up for a doozy, though. I had that exact thought last week.

Fuck!

I turn, desperate to take my frustration out on something, anything. I spot my lamp on my dresser. Just as I'm about to grab it and smash it, I hear the front door of my apartment squeak open. I might feel like utter shite that my relationship with Maddie is a product of my wayward magic, but that doesn't mean I'm about to sit here and let some bastard rob my apartment.

Besides, I'd rather smash a thief than break the only lamp in my bedroom. And I might. I'm so hurt and angry, I might just pummel any fool who's snuck into my home—until I stalk into the room and recognize the dark-hair tinged with grey and the bushy eyebrows framing a pair of eyes as green as mine.

"Dad?"

"Who else would it be, boyo?"

"What are you doing here? I thought you were in Ireland still."

The last couple of years, my parents always went home to Ireland for St. Patrick's Day, but they made a long vacation of it. I know I've been staying at Maddie's for quite some time. It's still March. I wasn't expecting to see my dad again until the first week of April at the earliest.

"What? And miss out on seeing my only son finally come into his own?"

I scowl. Come into my own? Yeah, right. I didn't learn how to use the magic. My magic fucking used *me.*

"What's wrong, Kill?"

"My luck. My rotten fuckin' luck, Dad. I thought I was fallin' for this girl, and the cupid even said I was, but now I know that my feelings aren't real. It's the amulet's fault. She wished for someone to love her and because of the geis, I had to grant her wish."

Finn's silent for a second. What can he say? Sorry? That won't help. Nothing will.

And then he nods.

"Sit down."

Really? "Dad, I don't want—"

"Sit!"

I sit. Moving over to my couch, I plop my ass down.

Clearing his throat, Finn says, "Did I ever tell you how I met your mother?"

Only a million times as I was growing up. Every holiday, every anniversary... hell, half the time when he had a couple of whiskeys too many, I heard the story. But since there's that steely look in my dad's green eyes that I recognize all too well, I keep my mouth shut. I nod.

"Did I ever tell you that she's the one who found my amulet?"

I blink. "Um. No. I think you might've left that part out."

"I had to. Like you said, it's part of the geis. The magic. And it's something every leprechaun who finds their mate goes through. The amulet's not only responsible for your magic, son, or even your luck. It's the token of your heart. It wasn't ever yours—it was just waiting for the woman it belonged to. The woman who would own your heart someday.

"So, aye, when you think it's the magic's fault that you love this lass, you're not all wrong. But you're not right, either. It's like your luck. You've not had bad luck all your life because you're half a leprechaun—there's no such thing as half. If you're a lad and you're a wee Faerie, you're a leprechaun. It's that simple since, time I told you: there's no such thing as a female leprechaun. My mam's human, just like your mother is. When I say you're half leprechaun, it's because you haven't met your soul mate yet. You haven't met the one who your amulet recognizes as yours."

It takes me a second to understand exactly what my dad is saying. When it finally sinks in, when I finally accept that Maddie found my amulet because she's meant to be mine, I sputter out loud. I don't even care that he fibbed about lady leprechauns; not when the only woman I want is human. Or that I always thought Finn calling my mother his soul mate was his sappy side coming out when he got a little too deep in his cups.

I only want to know one thing:

"Why didn't you tell me any of this before?"

"Two reasons, Kill. One, you had to learn it for yourself. Magic's all fine and dandy, but it's a good thing, the way it makes you work for everything you have. Your rotten luck was never all that bad, and if you could've snapped your fingers and had everything you wanted when you were a lad, you never would have grown up to be the man I know you are. Your amulet is a geis, it is. That's not all, though. It's your guide."

"It led me to my Maddie."

"Aye." Finn snaps his fingers, his amulet appearing between his thumb and his middle finger as soon as the *snap*ping sounds fades. A dimple pops in his cheeks as he lifts it high so I can see it. "Just like mine brought me to my Kathleen. People often joke about the luck of the Irish. You thought your heritage meant you were an unlucky sod. Not so. You've found your luck, my boy, in the arms of a good woman."

Now if that isn't some sappy shite, I don't know what is. But he's not wrong. Everything seemed to go right for me as soon as I followed my amulet to Salem. My luck turned the instant she let me stay with her, and things only got better the longer I was there.

And, once I've convinced her that she's meant to be mine, I'll be the luckiest bastard in Massachusetts.

"I have to get back to her, but my car's there." I run my hands anxiously through my hair. "I can take a cab but that'll take too long."

"Don't worry about it, Kill. You'll get control of your magic in time, be able to do all the tricks I can. For now, I'll help you. Get ready, figure out what you're going to do when you get back to your woman, then call me down at the bar. I'll get you to her, son."

"I owe you one, Dad. I really appreciate it."

He nods, then starts to leave. Something hits me as he goes and I call out to him.

"Dad, wait."

Finn turns around. He raises his bushy eyebrow. "Aye?"

"You said you had two reasons why you didn't tell me the truth about being a leprechaun. What's the other one?"

"Oh, that?" He laughs, a real hearty sound. "I'm a leprechaun. You're my son, and I love ya, but I couldn't help myself. It was far too much fun to keep the secret. And letting you look for a female leprechaun when they don't exist? Oh, your mother and I had a good laugh over that!"

I roll my eyes. Of course, Mom was in on the truth, too. Makes sense—she really is Finn's soul mate.

Just like Maddie is mine.

12

JUST LUCKY

Maddie

"*MEOW.*"

Stewie jumps onto my lap, shoving her face into my armpit, trying to get me to stroke her head. With a wistful smile, I do, scratching her right next to her ears just the way she likes. In my other hand, I'm still holding onto Killian's banana.

Daisy is sitting primly on her haunches, tail folded around the front of her paws. The white tip flicks anxiously back and forth. Unlike her rambunctious former kitten, Daisy isn't begging me for my attention.

She doesn't want *me*.

"I know, baby. I miss him, too."

"*Mrow.*"

It's only been a couple of hours since Killian

vanished. For the first hour or so, I expected him to come back. Sure, he was finally able to escape my house without having to be my shadow. I'd want to run as far away as fast as possible too if I was him. But I don't think I was expecting too much to think he'd maybe say goodbye before he left Salem.

Then, when another hour goes by, I realize that his coming back might be a little more difficult. Killian made it clear that, despite the whole three wishes deal, he can't really use any of his leprechaun magic. I got my three wishes and I can't deny that my last one was for him to go away.

And he did. But he didn't take anything with him.

His car's out front. It's the first thing I checked after I ran through the house, assuring myself he was really gone. There's no sign of Killian nearby, though his duffel bag is still in my room and his car is parked behind mine in the drive. So I know he has to come back eventually. Without a car, though, that might be a little difficult. He could take a taxi or an Uber, sure, but would he?

I keep on hoping so. And, the more I do, the more I think about what that means. I'd spent days hoping he'd go, then a few days more denying that what we had could never last. I just... I never thought he'd disappear in a flash like that. Especially since, by my count, I'm still missing a wish.

For about the hundredth time since he *pop*ped out of here, I mutter, "I wish Killian would come back."

As soon as the words are out of my mouth, my doorbell rings.

Did that... did that actually *work* this time?

Only one way to find out. Murmuring to Stewie to stay on the couch, I leave the banana on my cushion before standing up. I carefully step around Daisy. Her triangle-shaped ears are pricked, her head swiveling to look toward the front door.

Taking that as a good sign, I nearly jog across the room. I pause for a second to compose myself before taking a deep breath and throwing my front door open.

And there he is.

Okay. So I really didn't think that that would work. I'd hoped he'd be on the other side of the door, but I'm actually super surprised to see him standing there wearing his familiar red sweatshirt.

I step back to allow him to come inside.

He doesn't move.

"Killian? What are you—" I lean around him, searching the road. I don't see any other cars heading down my street so either he'd been out here a while or he didn't get a ride. I have to ask. "*How* did you get here?"

"Magic, of course."

That smirk. The cocky little smirk of his. God, I'm a sucker, because I fucking missed that smirk.

I'm so happy to see him, but he hasn't even made a move to come any closer to me. Tucking a lock of my hair behind my ear, I purposely hide how glad I am to see that he's returned. I've learned that, despite my rashly formed first impression, Killian Finnegan is a good man. I'm sure his sudden disappearance earlier bothered him as much as it did me. Whatever the reason we got thrown together—whatever mistakes might have been made due to the stress of it all—there's no pretending we didn't get... close these last few days. I don't think I'm out of line if I expect him to at least say goodbye before disappearing out of my life forever.

"You got your amulet back," I say, keeping my tone nonchalant.

Killian nods. "I did."

Jerking my thumb over my shoulder, gesturing where I left Daisy and Stewie guarding the banana, I tell him, "I got my wishes."

"Aye."

He's doing it on purpose. I can tell. I've gotten to know him pretty well and he's doing this—the smirk, the short answers, the way he's propped his hip against my door jamb while lingering on my porch—he's doing it all to wind me up. Fine. But I'm not going to give him the satisfaction of reacting.

I shrug. "So why did you come back then?"

The gleam in his bright green eyes dims a little. His

mouth twitches, a hint of a frown tugging his lips downward. Taking his hands out of his pockets, he crosses them over his wide chest. "Don't know if you noticed, but I left a couple of things behind."

My heart sinks. I'd never admit it to Killian, but if he told me he came back for me, I'd be putty in his hands. Silly, Maddie. I knew all along that he only came onto me because I was the only one around and, well, we both had needs. I was using him just as much as he was clearly using me.

Only, I was the sucker who fell for my, oh jeez, could I even call it a fuck buddy if we never really were friends? I mean, we weren't in the beginning, and I thought we might've bonded over my girls and the cat puzzle, but the way Killian's acting right now? I guess I was wrong.

"Oh. Uh—yeah. I guess you did have to leave rather suddenly." I can't look at him. Knowing that he's only come back because his stuff was here, not because he wanted to see me again... it sucks. It hurts to have him here knowing that, in a few moments, he'll be gone and not because the magic whisked him away.

I should be happy. I finally have my house back to myself. My unwanted houseguest has no reason to stay —and I can't think of one good reason to invite him to. Telling him that I've begun to fall for him these last few days is crazy.

"I didn't know if—or when, really—to expect you

back so I didn't touch any of your stuff. You have your keys so I couldn't move your car. Hang on. Give me a second and I'll get your clothes and shit."

"Don't worry about it, sweetheart. I know where everything is. I'll take care of it."

Sweetheart. I never would've thought I'd get used to him calling me Maddie, but that *sweetheart* barb stings. It's like we're right back at the start. Of course, we are. He has his amulet back, right?

"Fine," I say. And if there's a bit of a snappish tone to the word, who can blame me? "Let me know if you need anything."

Killian nods and, without even a backward glance, he heads for the stairs.

Since I don't want him to see how his easy breezy attitude is just about killing me here, I pretend like I wasn't sitting on my couch, moping with my cats and a damn banana. I have a sudden need to get the stupid yellow fruit out of my sight. Storming back over to my couch, I snatch at the banana angrily, spooking both Daisy and Stewie as I do.

Daisy lets out another plaintive *mew,* then sets off for the stairs. She's probably going to see what Killian is doing up there. Traitor.

Stewie follows at my heels as I march into the kitchen, throwing the magic banana into my freezer so that it doesn't get mixed in with any of my regular, non-magic fruit. Last thing I need is to make muffins or bread with it and have my baked goods be cursed or something.

Since Stewie is more loyal than her mother, I throw a couple of crunchy treats into her bowl. I leave Daisy's empty. She's going to have to make it up to me later if she wants treats. Trotting along after Killian? Did she forget who feeds her, brushes her fur, scoops her shitty litter box?

Humph. She's lucky if I don't pack her up and ship her off to Boston with Killian.

Speak of the devil. I barely have that thought when his voice rings out.

"Maddie? Where did you go?"

He must be done getting his crap together already. That was quick. He must be anxious to get out of here.

Now, I don't want to face him, but I also don't want to give him the satisfaction of knowing that I'm hiding somewhere in my own damn house. Stopping only to pat Stewie on her head and take some heart from my *loyal* companion, I straighten up and head back into my living room to face off with Killian.

And, holy crap, he's carrying Daisy's cat carrier.

Whoa. What is going on? Did he read my mind? Almost as soon as I truly accepted that he was a leprechaun, Killian explained the extent of his Faerie magic in order to convince me that he was harmless. Among the hundreds of questions I asked him as we worked on the puzzle, I distinctly remember asking him if mind-reading was one of his skills. Not even close. Apart from the wishes he owed me because I managed to stumble on his amulet, shrinking down to mini-Killian was the extent of his powers. I believed him because, well, what else could I do?

If it turned out he lied to me, I'll kill him.

Can you kill a leprechaun? I don't know, but I'll sure as hell find out!

"What are you doing?"

He glances at the cat carrier, then meets my fierce gaze. There's that sparkle in his bright green eyes that I've come to adore. It's his teasing expression, only there's something more there. Something honest, something pure. The smirk? It's gone. His smile is one part sweet, another part lascivious, and the second I see it, I lose most of my fury.

Because that smile? I know *that* smile. It's the smile he wears right before he goes down on me. When Killian licks his lips before answering me, I worry again that he can hear exactly what I'm thinking. If my thoughts aren't in the gutter, it's only because I'm thinking of his head between my thighs.

Right now? He might actually get a pass. I don't think I'd care that he kept that from me if he followed through on the sudden promise in his eyes. My heart starts to thump wildly—and that's not the only part of me that's affected. My panties are almost immediately damp, I want this man so badly.

"I told you I left a couple of things behind, right? If I'm bringing you and the girls home with me, I'm going to need carriers for them. I remember seeing this one in the corner of your room. Do you have another one? Or do I have to go out and grab one? It's big, but I want Daisy and Stew to be comfortable on the ride."

Wait— *what?*

My mouth drops open. Seriously. If it was possible, it would've been on the floor. Not my sexiest moment, for sure, but I can't help it.

Did he really just say that?

When I don't answer him—when I can't even *think* of anything to say in response to that—Killian continues.

"Unless you want me to stay here. It might be better. My apartment is kind of tight. The girls need their space, don't you think? My bed's a bit bigger, though. I've got a king, so maybe we can swap it out with yours. Plus my Sox pennant, I'll have to bring that with me. Other than that, I'm happy to live here with you. Just puttin' that out there."

"Live here?" I echo weakly. My heart's beating so fast, I can barely hear myself talk. "With me? What? *Why?*"

"You're kiddin', Maddie. Don't you know?"

"What's going on? Killian... okay, look I'm really confused right now, and I *hate* being confused. I thought you were gone—and now you're standing here, holding Daisy's carrier, talking about moving in. Did I miss something? I thought this was over with. You have your amulet. Isn't that enough? I... I really like you, Kill. Don't know why—"

He nods again, his grin creeping up a little higher as if he liked that, even if I'm kind of insulting him. "That's fair."

"Yeah, well, it's a shock to me, too. So, please, stop teasing me."

"Teasin'? Oh, Maddie, sweetheart. I'm not teasin'. I haven't been teasin' since the first time you let me in your bed. From that moment, it's become my goal to stay there. And it's not just the sex, though we both know it's mind-blowin'. It's you. Prickly and uptight and a wee bit anal-retentive, yeah, but you're perfect for me. Cats and all. So, of course, I want to stay."

From anyone else, I would think that was as much a load of shit as it was insulting. From Killian, that's the closest to a declaration of love as I'd ever expect.

I swallow the sudden lump in my throat. I have to ask. I have to be sure. "What... what are you saying?"

"See? That's another thing that should be annoyin', but it's you so I think it's fuckin' adorable. You've got this need to double- and triple-check every fact, like you can't believe half the things you're told. You let me stay here with you, I'm gonna see to it that you always know I'm tellin' you the truth."

He looks so determined, I stop second-guessing his

motives at that very moment. Because you know what? He's right. Killian is absolutely right.

"I already know that," I confess. As insecure and unsure as I am, I take a deep breath and move closer to him. "You've never lied to me."

That's the truth, too. Even when I wanted him to sugarcoat things, he never lied to me. So maybe, just maybe, he's being honest now.

I really fucking hope so.

I don't know what it is I did, whether it's my admission or something in the way I'm looking up at him, but something changes in Killian. Placing the cat carrier down on the floor, he crosses the distance and places his hands on my shoulders, forcing me to tilt my head all the way back so that I can look right in his face.

"So what's the answer, Maddie? My place or yours? Because, I'll tell you this, we're gonna be together. I know you like to be in charge, sweetheart, but I'm gonna have to insist on that. You already used up your wish to get rid of me, but the magic's mine again. Stronger, too, now. So if you want me to leave, you can ask, but I promise that I'll keep on comin' back here until you give us an honest go of it.

"Boston's only a half hour drive, and I can always commute between Finnegan's and here. Anything show you that I mean it. You won't be able to get rid of me, Maddie. Trust me, you've never seen anything until you've seen a leprechaun in love. We're worse than jock itch, we are."

Should I laugh? I don't know. I do anyway. Can't help it.

The last of my giggle is swallowed by Killian as he ducks his head, taking my chin in his hands and covering my lips with his. My mouth was open as I laughed. He takes advantage to deepen the kiss.

I'm out of breath when he finally breaks the kiss. He doesn't let go of me, using his thumbs to caress my cheeks gently. His gaze is narrowed intently on me, like he's either waiting for me to give in—or waiting for the chance to steal another kiss in order to try convincing me some more.

And then the last thing he said—before his joke about being worse than a contagious rash—slams into my dazed brain. *A leprechaun in love.* He couldn't actually mean that, could he?

Then again, he did say he would never lie.

I decide right then and there that, for probably the first time in my life, I'm not going to question it. He says he loves me? Considering that I'm more than halfway in love with him myself, I *want* to believe it. So I do.

I wanted a man to love, and a man who could love me in return. Does it matter that he's half leprechaun? Not to me.

So, taking a deep breath, I tell him, "If you're

willing to commute, you can stay here. You can stay with us." And then, because I like to tell the truth, too, I add, "I really hate driving in Boston."

It's his turn to laugh. And it's sexy and it's deep, a chuckle that starts in his chest and travels all the way down to his boots. He pulls back, letting go of me for a moment so that he can wrap his arms around my shoulders, pulling me into the warmth of his arms.

"You're one in a million, Maddie," Killian murmurs, the heat of his breath sending pleasurable shivers up and down my spine. If I even doubted him for a second, I wouldn't now. Pressed against him, his rock hard erection a signal of his lust, the rapid beat of his heart pounding against my chest proof that he also feels our connection... this is meant to be. This wasn't just a wish. It's fate. As if echoing my thoughts, he says, "I knew it, too. I knew from the minute you walked into Finn's that you were special."

"And I thought you were a condescending ass," I remember with a genuine smile. "I still can't figure out how you got me to change my mind."

Killian reaches his hand between us, placing his pointer finger beneath my chin in order to tilt my head back. An instant before he leans in and gives me another heated promise of a kiss, I hear his sexy Irish accent whisper, "Just lucky, I guess."

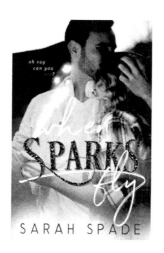

When sparks fly, it's all too easy to be burned...

Felicity

It seemed like the perfect job. My old high school was in need of an art teacher. I studied art in college.They were desperate.

I start in September.

Of course, that meant I had to leave my adopted city, trading New Jersey for Salem—even after I swore I would never return. Knowing I would need the summer to prepare, I moved back at the end of June, trying hard not to remember why I chose to stay away these last five years.

Emile Banks.

My high school sweetheart. The boy I used to love before he insisted on a "break" when I moved away to college. The man I can't stop picturing naked now that we met again at Salem High's Fourth of July celebration.

Ugh. Did he have to grow into such a gorgeous guy? Because he is. He's absolutely delicious and I've been starving for a long, long time.

But I promised myself years ago that I would never get mixed up with Emile again. The past was where it belonged—behind me. Only, it's kind of hard to believe that when he's standing in front of me, offering me the only thing I ever wanted.

Him.

Emile

Felicity Houston was the one who got away. My *if only*. My *I really screwed* that *one up*.

Our split was mutual. When high school ended and Felicity got accepted to a college in New Jersey while I stayed in Salem, we decided to break things off. We were high school sweethearts, each other's firsts in everything that counted, but I'd be lying if I said that I didn't want to see what else was out there. I was a stupid kid who was thinking with the wrong head because, within months of my first semester, I insisted the break become permanent.

By the time I realized that there was no one out there that I wanted more than Felicity, she'd already given up on me. She had moved on and she made it very clear that I needed to do the same. I promised I would—and that's when my brother got hit by a bus.

Zack was in a coma for two years. My love life got put on hold, I barely scraped by to earn my degree, and I spent all of my time keeping my family from falling apart. It was a miracle when Zack finally came out of his coma. It was an even bigger shock when he announced he was getting married within a month of leaving the rehab center. And it was a wake-up call that life can be over in an instant.If I want something?I have to go after it and take it.

Suddenly, after five years, Felicity is back in Salem. She got away from me once. This summer, I'm going to do everything I can to make her mine again.

When Sparks Fly is the sixth and final entry in the **Holiday Hunk** series. It's a steamy contemporary novella with enough fireworks to light up the Fourth of July! A second chance romance with a determined hero, a wary heroine, a cop with a very poor sense of timing, plus a very interesting trip to the summer movies.

** It's also a companion to **Halloween Boo.** The hero of this book is the brother of that one and some of the details referenced in this one are from that story. You'll definitely enjoy this one a little more if you've read that one.

Get it now!

After my mate rejected me, I wanted to kill him. Instead, I ran away—which nearly killed *me*...

A year ago, everything was different. I had just left my home, joining the infamous Mountainside Pack. The daughter of an omega wolf, I've always been prized -- but just not as prized as I would be if my new packmates found out my secret.

But then my fated mate—Mountainside's Alpha—rejects me in front of his whole pack council and my secret gets out, I realize I only have one option. Going lone wolf is the only choice I've got, and I take it.

Now I live in Muncie, hiding in plain sight. If the wolves ever left the mountains surrounding the city, I'd be in big trouble. Luckily, the truce between the vampires and my people is shaky at best and Muncie? It's total vamp territory. Thanks to my new vamp roomie, I get a pass, and I try to forget all about the call of the wolf. It's tough, though. I... I just can't forget my embarrassment—and my anger—from that night.

And then *he* shows up and my chance at forgetting flies out the damn wind.

Ryker Wolfson. He was supposed to be my fated mate, but he chose his pack over our bond. At least, he did—but now that he knows what I've been hiding, he wants me back.

But doesn't he remember?

I told him I'll never be his mate, and there isn't a single thing he can do to change my mind.

To Ryker, that sounds like a challenge. And if there's one thing I know about wolf shifters, it's that they can never resist a challenge.

Just like I'm finding it more difficult than I should to resist *him*.

---

* ***Never His Mate*** is the first novel in the *Claw and Fang* series. It's a steamy rejected mates shifter romance, and

though the hero eventually realizes his mistake, the fierce, independent heroine isn't the sweet wolf everyone thinks she's supposed to be...

Get it now!

KEEP IN TOUCH

Stay tuned for what's coming up next! Sign up for my mailing list for news, promotions, upcoming releases, and more!

Sarah Spade's Stories

And make sure to check out my Facebook page for all release news:

http://facebook.com/sarahspadebooks

Sarah Spade is a pen name that I used specifically to write these holiday-based novellas (as well as a few books that will be coming out in the future). If you're interested in reading other books that I've written (romantic suspense, Greek mythology-based romance, shifters/vampires/witches romance, and fae romance), check out my other author account here:

http://amazon.com/author/jessicalynch

Of Mistletoe and Mating

No Way

Season of the Witch

Rogue

Sunglasses at Night

Ain't No Angel *free*

True Angel

Ghost of Jealousy

Night Angel

Broken Wings

Lost Angel

Born to Run

Ordinance 7304: Books 1-3

Printed in Great Britain
by Amazon